LOVE'S RANSOM

WITHDRAWN

LOVE'S RANSOM

Dana James

Chivers Press • G.K. Hall & Co.
Bath, England   Waterville, Maine USA

This Large Print edition is published by Chivers Press, England, and by G.K. Hall & Co., USA.

Published in 2001 in the U.K. by arrangement with the Author c/o Dorian Literary Agency.

Published in 2001 in the U.S. by arrangement with Dorian Literary Agency.

U.K. Hardcover   ISBN 0-7540-4558-7   (Chivers Large Print)
U.K. Softcover   ISBN 0-7540-4559-5   (Camden Large Print)
U.S. Softcover   ISBN 0-7838-9476-7   (Nightingale Series Edition)

The text of this Large Print edition is unabridged.
Other aspects of the book may vary from the original edition.

Set in 16 pt. New Times Roman.

Printed in Great Britain on acid-free paper.

British Library Cataloguing in Publication Data available

Library of Congress Cataloging-in-Publication Data

James, Dana, 1944–
    Love's ransom / by Dana James.
        p. cm.
    ISBN 0-7838-9476-7 (lg. print : sc : alk. paper)
    1. Caribbean Area—Fiction. 2. Large type books. I. Title.
PR6060.A4527 L68 2001
823'.914—dc21   2001024196

This book is dedicated to Jill Harris.
With love and thanks.

CHAPTER ONE

Zanthi glanced up from her electric typewriter and smiled as her secretary set the tea-tray down on one corner of the vast, crowded desk. 'Margaret, you're an angel.' Leaning back in the swivel chair, she stretched her bare brown legs out in front of her, and her arms high above her head to ease the stiffness in her shoulders.

The tropical sun streamed in through the long windows, filling the high-ceilinged room with the golden light of late afternoon.

'You do know it's almost four-thirty?' Margaret Blaine reminded her. With thirty years' experience in the workings of Government House, a memory like an elephant, and a mouth as tight as a clam, she was invaluable to Zanthi.

'*What?*' Zanthi cried in dismay and sat bolt upright in her chair as she stared at her watch. '*It can't be.*' She sighed and sagged back once more, loosening her short-sleeved overshirt and matching skirt of black and white striped cotton where they clung to her sweat-dewed skin. 'When did they say the air-conditioning would be working again?'

'In time for the dinner tonight,' Margaret replied, adding drily, 'all being well.'

Zanthi made a face. 'Naturally.' She blew

1

her breath out in a soft sigh and stared at the files and papers covering her desk. 'I'll never get this lot finished today. I can't even work on tonight because of the dinner. That's the third official function I've had to attend this week.'

Carefully, Margaret set the fine, bone-china cup and saucer down within Zanthi's reach. 'Couldn't you get out of it just this once? You have had an awful lot of extra work lately.'

Zanthi pushed her slim hands through honey-brown hair cut close on her neck and gilded by the sunlight. She shook her head. 'No chance. Not this one. It's to launch the new mountain road scheme, and His Excellency has assigned me to look after this surveyor upon whom, apparently, the whole thing depends.' She raised her wing-like brows and shrugged. Lifting the cup, she cradled it in both hands, leaning her elbows on the desk. 'Not only have I to introduce him to the Ministers of Finance and Public Works and their ladies, and hang about while they all make polite conversation, I'm also supposed to have done enough homework to be able to show an intelligent interest in his work. Then, while making sure he circulates, I am to provide him with anything he asks for in the way of introductions and information.' She sighed again. 'With so much spare time perhaps I should knit him a hammock as well.'

With a sympathetic smile Margaret gathered up the files and newly typed letters

2

from the wire tray. 'Would you like me to take these up to Sir James for signing?'

Zanthi nodded. 'That would be a help. Most of them are official, from the Assembly to the Home Office. But some are personalised. Perhaps, if you could . . . a tactful reminder . . .?'

Margaret nodded. 'Don't worry. I'll make sure he knows which is which.' She leaned forward, lowering her voice to a confidential murmur. 'In my opinion, Lieutenant Benham is expecting far too much of you. Not that you aren't more than capable of doing the *work*. I didn't mean that. But you shouldn't *have* to be doing all this extra.'

Although Zanthi and her immediate superior were on first-name terms, she had never heard Margaret refer to the ADC by anything other than his rank and surname, a sure sign of her disapproval.

Draining the last of her tea, Zanthi replaced the cup on the saucer. 'That was a life-saver.' She handed it to her secretary. 'He has been very busy with errands for the Governor,' she offered by way of an excuse, recognising as she did so how Paul was using her loyalty and commitment to her job for his own ends.

Margaret snorted, drawing herself up so that her short, plump body, clad in neat navy skirt and cream silk blouse, resembled that of a pouter pigeon. She patted the silver regimented waves of her stiff perm. 'Very busy

3

making up to her ladyship is more like the truth of it,' she muttered.

'Margaret!' Zanthi was startled. It was a standing joke among everyone connected with Government House and Office that squeezing blood from a stone was easier than worming a secret out of Margaret Blaine. That this soul of discretion should have let slip such a remark revealed a deep concern that found an answering echo in Zanthi.

The building had been buzzing with rumours for weeks but, rushed off her feet, Zanthi had had no time to heed them. Even when, earlier that week, she had come upon the ADC and the Governor's wife unexpectedly, and had been struck by the rosy flush on Lady Fiona's plain features and the misty luminosity in her eyes, she had refused to read anything into it.

The fact that Paul had come to her office only minutes later, full of his usual banter, and asked her out, had also helped to dispel her brief uncertainty even though, as always, she had turned him down.

'If His Excellency gave as much time and attention to his wife as he does to that blessed, garden,' Margaret muttered, worry deepening the creases between her unplucked brows, 'Lady Fiona wouldn't be running the risk of making a fool of herself.'

'But what about Paul . . . Lieutenant Benham?' Zanthi looked up at her secretary.

'If it *is* true, and there is something going on, which I don't believe for a minute,' she added hastily, 'isn't *he* taking an awful chance?'

Margaret snorted again. 'I wouldn't worry about him.' Her mouth pursed in indignation. 'He knows exactly what he's doing. And he's making time for it by off-loading his work on to you.'

Zanthi was shaken. She had been so busy, she simply hadn't had time to realise how potentially serious the situation had become. Yet in her heart she recognised that this was only part of the problem. It was the other, broader aspect that worried her more.

She tried to make light of it, still clinging to the hope that Margaret was somehow mistaken. 'Paul is a charmer,' she shrugged. 'It's as natural to him as breathing. Perhaps her ladyship is simply flattered and is playing up to it a bit, just for a joke, a little light relief.'

Margaret's expression was that of someone who had walked in something unpleasant. 'Lieutenant Benham is charming, all right, when and with whom it suits him.'

Zanthi looked bemused. 'What are you trying to say?'

Margaret leaned closer and Zanthi caught a faint whiff of Devon Violets. The simple, old-fashioned scent was in such contrast to the atmosphere of conspiracy and intrigue that Zanthi was forced to hide a smile.

'The Governor's term of office finishes at

the end of the year. The new Governor will appoint his own ADC,' said Margaret. 'I think Lieutenant Benham is an ambitious young man who intends to move on from here with excellent references and a promotion, and he's leaving nothing to chance.'

Zanthi blinked. She started to smile, but it quickly faded, replaced by disbelief, then horror. 'You're joking.'

Margaret shook her head firmly. 'Oh no, I'm not. Lieutenant Benham is thirty-two. Lady Fiona is fifty-four years old, childless, and not even her closest friends would call her pretty. So what other reason could Lieutenant Benham possibly have for—' her rosy complexion darkened to brick-red—'carrying on with her the way he is?'

Automatically, Zanthi lowered her voice to match that of her secretary. 'Does Sir James know?' Her forehead furrowed as her mind ranged back over her recent meetings with the stooped, sparely built man, whose clipped speech and brusque manner hid a kindness which had endeared him to the islanders, and whose rare smile could light up a room.

Margaret hesitated a moment. 'If he does, he's keeping his thoughts on the matter very much to himself. But I don't believe he does know. In fact . . . well, it's not my place to say so, but,' one hand strayed to her hair again, 'His Excellency does seem to be a little . . . out of touch with things at the moment.'

'In what way?' The niggling anxiety which for weeks Zanthi had been trying to suppress sharpened her voice.

'Don't tell me you haven't noticed?' Margaret sounded surprised.

Zanthi sighed and, pushing her chair back, got up and walked over to the window which was opened top and bottom to catch any cooling draught.

Clasping her arms loosely across her midriff, she leaned one shoulder against the frame and gazed out on to the immaculate lawn. Clipped to carpet-smoothness, it resembled emerald baize and was edged with clusters of flowering shrubs. Their purple, yellow and cyclamen-pink flowers were splashes of vivid colour amid the rich green foliage and provided jewel-bright contrast to the cool shadows of the coconut palms.

'Yes,' she admitted. 'I've noticed, though I've tried to ignore it. I've been giving myself all sorts of reasons as to why he seems . . . withdrawn.'

'Well, if he doesn't know about her ladyship and Lieutenant Benham, perhaps it's something to do with the island that's on his mind?' Margaret suggested.

'I only wish it were,' said Zanthi softly. 'But, according to his reports to London, everything is just fine.'

Margaret looked concerned. 'You mean it isn't?'

Zanthi shrugged helplessly. 'I just don't know. It's only a feeling I've got, but—' She stiffened, straightening up, her eye caught by a movement in the shadows at the far side of the garden. 'Who is that? More to the point, what is he doing out there?'

The older woman hurried to her side. 'He's not staff,' she announced with certainty. 'So he has no business in His Excellency's garden. Where's that Dennis? It's his job to make sure no unauthorised person gets past the front entrance.'

Zanthi's mouth quirked in a wry grin. 'Our ex-Marine sergeant is probably regaling tonight's cadet guard of honour with tales of his exploits in some jungle or arctic waste.'

'Arctic wastes indeed,' Margaret sniffed. 'He's another one could do with keeping his mind on his job.' Clasping the files and correspondence firmly to her bolster-like bosom, she marched to the door.

'Now, Margaret,' Zanthi teased gently, 'don't be too hard on him. You know he's terrified of you.'

'I'll give him terrified,' promised Margaret grimly. 'He doesn't know he's born yet.' She closed the door behind her with a sharp click.

Zanthi turned once more to look out of the window, her smile fading. He certainly wasn't a burglar. Nor did he have the half-apologetic, half-defiant air normally exhibited by tourists whose passports had gone astray and who had

8

been sent up to Government Office to obtain a temporary replacement.

In fact, as he emerged fully from the shadows and stood at the edge of the lawn, scanning the building with a slow sweeping glance, he looked far more relaxed than she felt, and Zanthi found that oddly annoying.

The jacket of his beige lightweight suit was slung over his shoulder, hooked on one finger. His other hand was pushed casually into his trouser pocket. His shirtsleeves were turned back half-way up deeply tanned forearms. He had unfastened his collar and loosened his tie. Tall, dark-haired, broad-shouldered, and long-limbed, with a fluid stride that covered the ground deceptively fast, he started across the lawn at an angle which, within seconds, would take him out of view.

Where was Dennis? Or Sir James's chauffeur? Hadn't *anyone* noticed the intruder?

Acting purely on impulse, Zanthi whirled from the window and ran out of the office, down the short corridor and across the hall, her sandalled feet slapping against the tiled floor.

He was probably harmless and no doubt had a dozen excuses, but he had no right to be in the garden. This was just one more example of the way things had slipped recently.

As she burst through the fire door on to the flagged path, Zanthi stumbled to a breathless and undignified halt, barely avoiding a collision.

The man looked down at her. His black brows were almost straight, but the left one had a slight curve which gave him an air of quiet irony. 'Where's the fire?' His voice, a deep, throaty bass, reminded her of distant thunder.

At five foot seven, Zanthi had always thought of herself as reasonably tall, but she had to tilt her head backwards to meet his gaze.

Fringed with black lashes, his eyes were the colour of dark chocolate and observed her steadily without a trace of embarrassment.

A broad deep forehead, strong straight nose and well-defined cheekbones added to the overall impression of solid strength. Only his mouth, wide and mobile, with a slightly fuller bottom lip, hinted at the possibility of gentleness and humour.

'There isn't . . . I mean, that's not . . .'

'*Oi, you there,*' Dennis's bull-like roar cut across Zanthi's flustered explanation as he pounded towards them.

'Please excuse me, Miss . . .?' He paused, the curved brow raised in enquiry.

'Fitzroy,' Zanthi responded automatically.

'It appears I'm wanted.'

'You shouldn't be here,' she blurted, trying to regain control of a situation which seemed unaccountably to be in his hands.

10

'On the contrary,' he replied quietly, but, before she could ask him what he meant, he added, 'I believe I hear your telephone.'

Zanthi glanced over her shoulder and as she turned back he was already walking away to meet Dennis. She was furious at the ease with which he had distracted her. Torn between joining Dennis for the pleasure of seeing the man taken down a peg or two, and the possibility that her phone was ringing, duty won, and she hurriedly returned to her office.

As she reached the door, she could hear the bell. Dashing in, she snatched up the receiver. 'Hello? Assistant Secretary here.' How could he have heard it? The fire door had shut behind her. The husky tones of the Governor's wife came over the line. 'No, ma'am, Lieutenant Benham isn't here at the moment.' She glanced at her watch. 'I'm expecting him any time within the next half-hour. Yes, ma'am, I'll tell him.' Zanthi replaced the receiver, her expression thoughtful.

Sitting down at her desk, she rubbed the back of her neck, feeling the muscles taut, and knotted. A deep, shuddering sigh revealed her weariness and growing confusion.

How many times, during those drab winter days in England when even the air was cold, grey and lifeless, had she dreamed of coming home to Jumelle, where Atlantic rollers driven by the north-east tradewinds crashed on to the rocky eastern shores, foaming over black,

11

volcanic sand that glistened like a star-spangled night sky? Whose western coast was lapped by the limpid, turquoise waters of the Caribbean, and whose endless beaches of powder-fine, white sand were shaded by tall coconut palms? But now she was home, nothing was as she had imagined it would be.

She loved her job and knew she was good at it, so the problem didn't lie with her work. No, that wasn't entirely true. It was her decision to apply for the post at Government House through the Diplomatic Service which had caused the rift with her patents.

Zanthi had clung to the hope that, after their initial disappointment at her refusal to return to the suffocating insularity of plantation life, her family would eventually understand her reasons. But that hope was fading fast.

Her mind flew back to her last visit home three weeks ago. It was etched in her brain, as sharp and clear as if it had been yesterday. She hadn't wanted another row. She had done everything she could to avoid it. But her father had clearly been determined to assert his authority.

'Well, Zanthi?' He had glared down the length of the table, past her two brothers and their wives, to where she sat next to her mother. 'When are you going to give up this nonsense and come back home where you belong?'

12

'I wouldn't call working at Government House nonsense,' she replied evenly.

'Glorified paper-pushing, that's all it is,' Steven Fitzroy grunted impatiently.

Zanthi hung on to her temper as all heads turned her way. The simultaneous movement reminded her of spectators at a tennis match and, involuntarily, she smiled.

'I don't see anything to laugh at, miss,' he snapped. 'I see ingratitude and selfishness. I see you indulging your own wishes with no thought of your obligation to this family. There have been Fitzroys on this plantation for three hundred years. All of us have a responsibility, a duty to our heritage, and that includes you.'

Hot with anger and embarrassment at being spoken to as though she were a wilful child, rather than a woman of twenty-four, Zanthi was also acutely aware of the mixed resentment and speculation on the faces of her sisters-in-law. Her father had deliberately engineered this confrontation, she realised, hoping to shame her into submission. For the sake of her own self-respect she could no longer turn the other cheek.

Crumpling her napkin and laying it beside her plate, Zanthi faced her father, her chin high. 'Tell me, why did you insist on sending me to an expensive English boarding-school and then on to university with the express purpose of encouraging me to use my brains and think for myself, if you now intend to deny me any independence? What you are attempting, Father, is emotional blackmail, and I will not submit to it. My life is my own, to live as I want.'

'Then do it and be damned!' he had roared, and stalked off to his study.

At her desk now, Zanthi rolled her head from side to side, her eyes closed. She might as well face it: the situation with her father had reached deadlock and there was no one else to whom she could turn for comfort or advice.

Her mother was growing steadily weaker. The doctors could not pin down the cause of her debility. Her body frail and desiccated, her skin lined like fine parchment, Madeline Fitzroy was withering away. Zanthi wondered sometimes if her mother had been simply overpowered by the lushness of the steaming jungle that clothed the mountains and lurked at the edge of the plantation, kept at bay only by constant vigilance and back-breaking toil.

Unable to tolerate stress, Madeline refused to acknowledge it. She simply blocked out anything unpleasant.

Many times Zanthi had gone back to the plantation on holiday from school, or during university vacation, longing to confide in her mother and talk through things that had happened. The business with Jeremy had shaken her to the core. But neither the time, the atmosphere, nor the state of her mother's

14

health had ever seemed right. The quarrel with her father had set her even further apart from the family.

As she cupped her chin on her palms, realisation washed over Zanthi: to all intents and purposes, she was entirely alone.

Since her return to the island, the demands of her job had given her little time to make new friends. In any case, an attractive, intelligent, single twenty-four-year-old without a fiancé or even a permanent boyfriend represented far too much of a threat to be welcome at private parties, except to make up numbers as a partner for an extra man.

At first she had been happy to accept these invitations, hoping to expand her social life beyond the receptions, cocktail parties and dinners she was obliged to attend as part of her job. But it soon became unpleasantly clear that she too was considered part of the menu, and that her partners expected more than mere conversation. From then on, hiding her hurt and disgust behind a polite smile, she pleaded pressure of work or a previous engagement, and went swimming or walking instead.

The door opened suddenly, making her jump. 'Oh,' she blew a small sigh of relief, 'it's you! I wish you'd knock or cough or something, Paul. You just *appear*. I never even hear your footsteps. It's unnerving.'

'What's this? You've got something to

15

hide?' The ADC flashed an arch grin at her. A couple of inches under six feet, he had a stocky frame which was beginning to show signs of softness at the waist and beneath the chin. But the lock of fair curly hair that had fallen across his forehead gave him a boyish look that belied his real age. Though today he was wearing civilian clothes, his fawn trousers and pale blue short-sleeved shirt were as crisply pressed as his dress uniform. 'There are few secrets in this place. Surely you've learnt that in the two years you've been here?'

Zanthi stiffened. Pulling forward a new batch of files, she picked up two fresh sheets of paper, slotted a carbon between them and rolled them into her typewriter. 'Maybe it would be better if there were one or two more,' she murmured. She hadn't really intended to say it aloud.

For several seconds Paul was quite still and Zanthi could almost *hear* his mind racing. Then his grin widened. He leaned down, placing one hand on the back of her chair while the other rested flat on the desk, and she was enveloped by the sweet, heady scent of his aftershave.

'Can it be that you're jealous, Zanthi?' His roguish tone did not entirely mask a note of shrewdness.

It was on the tip of her tongue to tell him not to be ridiculous. But she stopped herself in time. Knowing Paul Benham as she did, she

16

realised he would read a curt retort not as irritation at his conceit, but as an acknowledgement of his truth. She couldn't allow that. Clenching her teeth, she shot him a glance of brief enquiry, 'Jealous of what, Paul?' she asked coolly.

He assumed an expression of exaggerated surprise. 'You mean you haven't heard the rumours?'

Zanthi turned back to her typewriter and, opening the top file, scanned the notes she had attached to the letter. She could swear he sounded slightly peeved. 'I don't have time to listen to gossip, Paul,' she replied pointedly. Her hands fell silent. 'Except . . .'

'Yes?' he prompted, his face only inches from hers.

'About the demonstrations down in Arlington . . .'

'What demonstrations?' he cut in derisively. 'A few youths waving banners?' He straightened up and pushed a hand through his hair in a gesture of mild impatience. Zanthi noticed that he carefully avoided disturbing the curl that fell over his forehead. It hadn't occurred to her before just how vain he was.

'So you don't think there's any connection between the Governor's . . . vagueness and the unrest in the town?' She regarded him calmly.

'What *unrest*?' he scoffed. But she noted the swift play of expressions across his well-tanned face. As his fair brows climbed

17

and his mouth stretched in a condescending grin, Zanthi was ironically amused to glimpse a new respect in his eyes. 'Look, Sir James is only a few months off retirement. It's perfectly natural that he should be slowing down a bit. After all, that's, what *I'm* here for, to take some of the load off him. As for the other—' He made a scornful, dismissive gesture. 'People complain. It's a law of nature. What would life be without a protest rally or two? But it's nothing to get excited or worried about.'

Zanthi rose from her desk and crossed to one of the grey metal filing cabinets. 'I hope you're right.' She wanted to believe him. 'Only . . . well, for what it's worth, I have a hunch something is brewing. I don't know what,' she added quickly to forestall any questions. 'And I don't know why . . . yet. It's just a feeling.'

Paul moved towards her. 'Do you know what I think?' He tried to slide his arm around her waist.

Side-stepping neatly out of reach, Zanthi tugged the drawer open and it shot out on well-oiled runners, forcing Paul to leap backwards. 'I'm sure you are about to tell me.'

'I think that as far as the island is concerned your imagination has gone into overdrive. You know why? Boredom.'

Zanthi glanced up from the filing drawer. 'I'm not bored, Paul. I love Jumelle. That's why I came back. It's my home.'

But he wasn't to be deflected. 'Apart from the rain, the biggest problem in this so-called tropical paradise is boredom.' He gave a gusty sigh.

'Perhaps that says more about you than it does about Jumelle,' remarked Zanthi sweetly and, slamming the drawer shut, she returned to her chair.

Paul hitched one hip on to the edge of her desk. 'Could be. However, there are ways to deal with it, and I'd like to suggest—'

The internal phone rang. 'Excuse me,' Zanthi broke in, and lifted the receiver.

'If that's Sir James,' whispered Paul, 'tell him—'

'Assistant Secretary's office,' she said into the mouthpiece. 'Yes, sir. Would you like to speak to . . .?' She listened, for several moments, a tiny frown appearing between her wing-like brows. 'Yes, sir, I'll tell him. Yes, right away.' She replaced the receiver slowly and looked up at Paul. 'The Governor would like you to go into Arlington and collect the invitations for the Spring Ball.'

'For God's sake, why *me*?' Paul glowered as his irritation boiled over. 'He could send his chauffeur. Damn it, there are enough people hanging about doing nothing.' He caught her eye and fell silent. After a second or two he shrugged, but Zanthi sensed the effort it cost him. 'Well, I suppose it is an important occasion,' he said at last. 'It's only natural His

19

Excellency should take a personal interest in the arrangements.'

'Yes,' Zanthi murmured. 'Of course.' She rubbed her arms, slowly as unease feathered over her skin, making it crawl. Something was undeniably wrong.

'Tell you what, why don't I come and pick you up?'

'What?' She looked blank.

'For the dinner tonight,' he said patiently.

Zanthi muffled a groan. She had forgotten about that. 'No, thank you. I may have to come early and I've no idea what time I'll be leaving. It all depends on this surveyor.' She looked swiftly around her desk. 'Oh, my God, where have I put his file?'

'That reminds me, I haven't seen your new place yet,' Paul said hopefully.

'No,' agreed Zanthi, still rummaging among the papers covering her desk.

'One of these days you'll weaken,' he promised, starting towards the door.

'Don't hold your breath,' she retorted lightly.

He reached for the door-handle. 'Honestly, Zanthi, it isn't natural, or healthy, for a gorgeous creature like you to live like a hermit.'

'You don't know how I live,' she pointed out, not bothering to look up.

'Rumour has it you don't like men.'

'Ah, rumour.' She smiled wryly. She could

sense his gaze on her, curious and irritated. They had had this conversation many times before and she had no intention of changing her mind and going out with him.

Zanthi knew perfectly well the only reason he kept asking was that she kept refusing. One day it would dawn on him that his persistence only strengthened her resolve, and he would stop wasting his time. Meanwhile, though at times his behaviour was a nuisance, it was also helping restore her confidence both in herself as a woman, and in her right to say no without explanation or apology.

It was three years since Jeremy and the scars had almost healed. Almost. She had been out with other men. But not Paul. There was something about Paul which reminded her of Jeremy, a smooth, surface charm which overlaid a deep, dark core of selfishness.

She recalled Margaret's muttered suspicions. Could he really be that callous and cynical?

'Don't knock rumour,' Paul chided. 'It's amazing what you can learn from the grapevine.'

If you only knew, Zanthi thought silently. Didn't he realise his behaviour was attracting speculation? Maybe he did and simply didn't care. He enjoyed the spotlight and had total confidence in his ability to think on his feet.

'In that case, if the grapevine is so reliable, why don't you know more about what's behind these protests?' Zanthi kept her voice light. She didn't want to antagonise him, or put him on the defensive. But she was genuinely perturbed.

'These protests,' he said with heavy patience, 'if you insist on calling them that, are nothing more than democracy in action. Besides,' he shrugged, pushing the whole business aside as a minor inconvenience, 'it's up to the Assembly to deal with. They are the elected representatives of the people. I've got far more important things to concern myself with.'

Like buttering up the Governer's wife? Zanthi tried to smother the thought, and breathed a sigh of relief as she located the pink folder. Sensing he would only get angry if she pressed further, Zanthi deliberately changed the subject. 'Do you know anything about him?'

'Who?'

She glanced at the name on the folder. 'Andrew Hemmings.'

Paul looked blank. 'Who?'

'The surveyor I'm assigned to look after this evening.'

'Oh, *him*. His name isn't Hemmings, it's Crossley, Garran Crossley.'

Zanthi stared at the folder. 'Then why—? Is there another folder?'

Paul made a gesture of irritation. 'How should I know? That's your province. All I

22

know is that the chap who was coming cried off through illness. This fellow Crossley is a replacement. There was a letter from the Overseas Development Administration. You must have it there somewhere.' He indicated her littered desk and frowned. 'Are you finding the work too much for you, Zanthi?'

Beneath the apparent solicitude Zanthi sensed a barb, like the poisonous spines of a sea-urchin camouflaged by a thin layer of sand. Paul did not take kindly to rejection at any level.

'I have no problems with the work itself,' she replied evenly. 'Though the amount does seem to have increased suddenly. However, it's nothing Margaret and I can't handle. I realise how difficult it must be for you.'

Suspicion flickered across his face. 'Difficult? For me? What are you talking about?'

'All this running about after Lady Fiona,' Zanthi replied innocently. 'No one would think she had a private secretary of her own, the demands she's making on your time. By the way, she rang down earlier. I was to ask you to go and see her as soon as you got back.'

Paul glanced at his watch. 'Why didn't you tell me sooner?' he demanded irritably.

'One, you didn't give me the chance, and two, I didn't realise it was so important,' Zanthi's tone was crisp.

He started to say something, changed his

mind and wrenched open the door.

'Don't forget the invitations,' Zanthi reminded him.

'What?' He glanced back over his shoulder. 'Oh, yes, right.'

'No rest for the wicked,' Zanthi smiled sweetly. Heaving a sigh as the door closed, she tossed the useless folder into the wire basket for Margaret to file and began to hunt for the ODA letter. Maybe, just maybe, it would tell her something about the man she was due to spend the evening with.

CHAPTER TWO

If there was a prize for the fastest shower and change of clothes, Zanthi thought as she clipped on discreet pearl earrings and turned to survey herself in the long mirror on the inside of her wardrobe door, she would have wiped out all the competition this week.

She sighed as she cast a critical eye over her reflection. Her thick, shiny hair needed little care, thank heaven. A thorough brushing had given the stylish cut body and bounce. It curved neatly into her neck, revealing the lower half of her small ears, and enhanced the size and upward tilt of her sea-green eyes.

A touch of blusher on her high cheekbones and a swift application of peach gloss to her full lips and she was just about ready.

Adjusting the tie-belt of her beige silk crêpe de Chine dinner dress, Zanthi pulled a wry face. She looked perfect, neat and unobtrusive. Colourless and nondescript was a more accurate if less flattering description. She shrugged at her reflection. The dress fulfilled all the demands of protocol: long sleeves, a high neckline and a subdued colour. She had to blend into the background. She smiled ironically. If she blended any further, she'd be invisible. Still, this was work, not pleasure.

Shutting the wardrobe door, she turned towards the bed and picked up from the flower-sprigged coverlet the small beige clutch bag that matched her dress and low-heeled court shoes. The taxi she had ordered would be here any minute to whisk her back to Government House.

While Margaret had combed the files, Zanthi had checked through every item on her desk in the hope of finding some background information on Garran Crossley. They had both drawn a complete blank. That in itself was odd. But Zanthi was already under so much pressure she forced herself to ignore the nagging suspicion that there was something strange about the last-minute substitution. After all, no one could help falling ill. It wasn't something one *chose*. In any case a new mountain road was hardly a security risk, so why should it matter who replaced Andrew

Hemmings?

As a last resort she had rung the public library in Arlington and persuaded the librarian to read the entry on land surveying in the careers encyclopaedia over the phone to her, while she hastily scribbled notes.

Throwing lipstick, hanky and comb into her bag, plus her taxi fare which she would reclaim from petty cash, she scanned the sheet of paper. Closing her eyes, she tried to commit some of the facts to memory. But her mind was awash with all that had happened during the day, as well as things she had to remember for the morning.

Refolding the paper, she thrust it into her bag. She would try to study it more carefully in the taxi. She snapped the bag shut and walked swiftly out into the living-room.

Half of one wall was taken up by sliding glass doors that opened on to a small private patio. These stood open and the frangipani, jasmine and honeysuckle festooning the open stonework which divided the patio from the one next door, filled the room with their delicious perfume.

The patio overlooked the garden and swimming pool shared by the six apartments in the old colonial house. Casting a longing glance at the pool, its clear water a sheet of shimmering blue silk, Zanthi wished she had had time for a swim.

It was one of her favourite forms of

exercise. The sensation of cool water caressing her limbs as she powered up and down the pool in a racing crawl never failed to soothe her mind, and the physical effort discharged all the tension that built up during hectic, demanding days. When she emerged she was relaxed, refreshed, and ready for her evening meal. But tonight there simply hadn't been a moment to spare.

Reluctantly, she closed the patio doors and turned to face the room. She drew in a deep breath of satisfaction, the corners of her mouth lifting.

Dark brown floor tiles gleamed with a rich patina of polish, and cream walls provided a perfect backdrop for the framed watercolours she was collecting of the island's exotic flowers.

There were cream rugs on the floor and a glass-topped coffee-table held a pile of magazines and a ceramic vase of flame-coloured lilies. The rattan-framed sofa and armchairs had thick, squashy cushions covered in a muted, floral print of dark blue, grey and rust, repeated in the curtains on either side of the patio doors.

Zanthi felt a little thrill of pleasure. There was still a lot to do. All her books lay in boxes behind the sofa, and her music centre sat on the floor in a corner. But once she had some shelves up the apartment really would look like a permanent home.

Turning back to flip the catch which would lock the glass doors, Zanthi hesitated for a moment, her gaze reaching beyond the garden, past the town nestling into the lush green hillside below and to her right, and out across the calm waters of the Caribbean, pewter beneath the orange and gold glory of the setting sun.

A sudden shiver raised gooseflesh on her arms and she caught her breath. But before she had time to puzzle out what had provoked the reaction, the doorbell rang. That would be her taxi. She offered up a silent prayer that the engineers would have got the air-conditioning working in time for the guests' arrival. There would be more than enough hot air generated in Government House this evening without any additional contribution by the climate.

Scooping up her keys from beside the telephone on the hall table, Zanthi dropped them into her bag and opened the door.

She gave a violent start and gulped. It wasn't the taxi-driver. It was the man she had seen from her office window. Only now, instead of the casual, almost dishevelled figure in shirtsleeves, jacket slung over his shoulder, the tall man standing barely two feet away looked strikingly handsome in a beautifully cut dinner jacket and black bow tie.

The stark contrast between dark trousers and dazzling white jacket emphasised the healthy tan on his rugged features and, though

28

his smile was formal rather than friendly, his eyes had a lazy, feral gleam which sent unease sliding like an icicle down her spine.

Zanthi stared at him, speechless.

'Hello again, Miss Fitzroy.' The deep, quiet voice made her toes curl.

'What do you want?' she managed at last, desperately trying to gather her wits. The initial shock was wearing off and her mind was beginning to function properly once more, though the impact of his sheer physical presence was even greater now than when she had almost collided with him on the path.

The curving left brow lifted fractionally, giving his smile a mocking edge. 'I've come to take you to dinner,' he announced calmly.

Zanthi's swift intake of breath made a soft hissing sound. 'I *beg* your pardon?' It had to be a joke. Someone was having a laugh at her expense. *But who?* It couldn't be Paul. He wouldn't set up another man in a situation he had aspired to and failed: he was far too vain.

It certainly wasn't Margaret. She had been genuinely angry and indignant at the stranger's sudden appearance in the garden. In her eyes rules were rules and there to be observed whether you liked them or not. If the Archangel Gabriel himself arrived at Government House without an appointment or a proper invitation, Margaret would send him packing. This wasn't her sense of humour.

So who else could it be? Zanthi realised she

had come full circle. There was no one else.

He made a slight movement with one shoulder, too brief to be an apology. 'I'm aware this is not the way things are usually done, but special circumstances call for special measures. By the way, I took the liberty of sending your taxi away. With a tip of course,' he added. 'The driver was quite happy.'

'You did *what*?' Zanthi's voice rose an octave.

'Well, we won't need two,' he pointed out reasonably. 'We can go right away if you wish. However, I was rather hoping we might have time to talk for a few minutes first.'

Zanthi had to swallow hard before she could get a word out. 'I don't believe this,' she murmured incredulously. 'You turn up on my doorstep, a total stranger, and expect me to go out to dinner with you?'

'Well, it is all arranged,' he began. 'I thought the introductions—'

'Then you can just *re*arrange it,' she interrupted curtly. But before she could say more he raised one hand to silence her and Zanthi couldn't help noticing that despite the squareness of his palm, suggesting strength and capability, his fingers were long and tapering.

'I wish I could, believe me,' he sounded as though he really meant it, 'but I'm afraid that is outside my power.'

Zanthi felt her anger crushed by growing

30

bewilderment, disquiet and, she had to admit, curiosity. 'Look, who *are* you? What's going on? Who put you up to this?'

'What a strange question, Miss Fitzroy.' He looked mildly puzzled. 'You know why I'm here. As you and I were destined to meet anyway, and my hotel is barely a few yards down the road, it seemed only sensible to . . .'

'What do you mean,' Zanthi cut in, feeling oddly breathless, 'destined to meet anyway?'

'Tonight, Miss Fitzroy,' his half-smile was gently mocking, 'at Government House.' He extended his hand. 'My name is Crossley, Garran Crossley.'

Zanthi flinched as though she had been struck, and a tiny, strangled sound escaped her lips. Embarrassment flooded her face with fiery colour, but at the same instant her anger returned in full force. He had deliberately set out to confuse and unsettle her, she was certain of it. But *why*?

Forcing herself to take the proffered hand, acutely aware, in spite of her indignation, of the warmth of his strong grip and the pressure of his long brown fingers, Zanthi lifted her chin and met his gaze. 'Perhaps if you had introduced yourself at once, Mr Crossley,' her tone crackled with frost, 'we might not have wasted so much time.'

He released her hand and it felt strangely cold now it was no longer enclosed in his. 'My time is valuable, Miss Fitzroy,' he answered,

31

his coolness matching hers. 'I never waste it.'

Zanthi's brain was working at top speed. So there was a reason behind his unorthodox greeting. *What was it?* 'May I ask what special circumstances you were referring to?' she enquired, her outward calm light-years away from the chaos of her thoughts.

She could feel tension tightening her muscles as all the implications started to become clear. She had not been due simply to *meet* Garran Crossley, she was to be his partner and escort for the entire evening.

There was a sudden hollowness in the pit of her stomach as she realised there would be no escape for at least the next three hours. They would be seated together at dinner, and protocol as well as good manners demanded she be an amusing, attentive and informative companion.

She wondered for a fleeting moment at her choice of the word 'escape'. Did she feel trapped? Not exactly. But she had never met anyone like him before, and so had no previous experience upon which to draw.

Already weary, she had known this evening would demand a lot from her, but she had had no warning of just how much.

So be it. It was part of her job and she would do it to the best of her ability.

'Do you enjoy your work, Miss Fitzroy?'

The question, following so closely the trend of her own thoughts, made her jump. 'Yes, most of the time.' Let him make what he liked of *that*. 'Do you enjoy yours?'

If he wanted to spar all evening he'd find her more than a match. But suddenly she hoped that he didn't. The pressures of the last few months were taking their toll. And the amount of concentration and nervous energy she would need to maintain such a façade would just about exhaust her.

'Most of the time.' He grinned suddenly and it was like looking at a different person, altogether more gentle and approachable. 'I wasn't poking fun,' he assured her, 'I really mean it. I loathe being stuck in an office. Fieldwork is what I enjoy most.'

She could understand that. He needed freedom and space. Confined behind a desk he would be like a caged tiger. She lowered her eyes quickly. How could she possibly make such an assumption? She knew nothing at all about him. Yet she was right, she would stake her life on it.

'Much as I am enjoying our conversation, Miss Fitzroy, I do feel that your doorstep lacks something in the way of ambience. May I take you somewhere for a drink?' There was an undercurrent of teasing laughter in his deep voice. 'To break the ice?'

Zanthi glanced up. His expression was studiously polite, but his dark eyes gleamed. Some of the tension went out of her. 'I wish we could.' The wistfulness in her voice startled her and she went on hurriedly, 'But I really think we ought to—'

'Correct me if I'm wrong,' he interrupted smoothly, his tone one of mild puzzlement, 'but I understand functions at Government House involve certain formalities. Isn't that right?'

Zanthi nodded.

'And these same formalities require that as my assigned escort for the evening it is your duty to ensure that my wishes are met?'

She nodded again, a little more slowly, sensing something behind his bland questions. *Questions to which he already knew the answers.*

'If it is within my power,' she replied evenly. 'Provided of course that your wishes relate to professional matters and are not merely personal indulgence.'

He leaned forward slightly. The movement was minimal but the implied threat made her heart beat faster. 'Are you questioning my integrity?' he demanded softly.

With a supreme effort she held his gaze, refusing to allow her lashes to fall and shield her from the laser-like probing. But her mouth was bone-dry and she had to swallow before she could reply.

'What can you mean, Mr Crossley? You asked me a question, I gave you an answer.'

'Then let me put it this way,' he smiled, his voice still deceptively gentle. 'Is it likely the ODA would send me all over the world to work on my own initiative in difficult locations and politically sensitive areas if I couldn't be trusted to keep my mind on my job?'

Zanthi felt hot colour stain her cheeks.

'Or,' he went on relentlessly, his mouth still smiling while his eyes glittered, their expression unreadable, 'do you have such faith in your attractiveness that you imagine every man you meet wants to bed you?'

Zanthi gasped, her eyes widening with shock. She couldn't have been more shaken if he had hit her. It took every ounce of strength to remain absolutely still and silent as she battled not only with inexplicable tears, but also with the almost irresistible urge to slap his face with all her strength and then to flay him verbally. She wanted so badly to make him cringe under a tongue-lashing he would never forget that she could almost taste it.

But something held her back. It wasn't just her diplomatic training, backed up by self-restraint. Something didn't add up. The feeling was based purely on intuition and was too nebulous for her to grasp. But Zanthi had learnt to listen to the quiet inner voice of her sixth sense and to trust her instincts. There was no time now, but she would not sleep tonight until she had identified what it was about Garran Crossley's behaviour that didn't ring true.

Meanwhile, the fact that there might be a reason for his rudeness didn't mean she had

35

simply to accept it. She tilted her chin. 'You seem determined to misunderstand me, Mr Crossley, though why I can't imagine. However,' she made a dismissive gesture, 'your hang-ups are none of my business.'

His eyes narrowed and his lips compressed momentarily. Zanthi felt her nerves tighten another notch, but refused to be intimidated.

'We both have a job to do. Provided we keep our personal prejudices to ourselves we should be able to survive the brief time we are forced to spend in each other's company.'

'So,' he mused softly, his gaze sweeping downwards from the top of her head to her shoes and back again, 'the kitten has sharp claws.'

Suddenly resentful of the pallid image she knew she presented, Zanthi hung on to her temper. 'Outward appearances can be very misleading, Mr Crossley,' she replied. 'You might find it useful to remember that. And just for the record,' her eyes flashed green fire, 'so there are no further *misunderstandings*, I am particularly careful in my choice of friends.'

'Ah,' he said slowly, nodding. 'How wise. It's always painful when trust is abused. But if it teaches you to choose quality rather than quantity, then the experience was worthwhile even if the result is occasional loneliness.'

Zanthi gaped at him, shaken. *How did he know?* She felt horribly vulnerable, as though all her defences had been torn down, leaving her naked and unprotected. He *couldn't* know. She had never told anyone here about Jeremy.

Realising her continued silence was itself a betrayal, Zanthi tried to pull herself together: Was this all part of some plan to keep her off-balance? But why would he want to do that?

'I enjoy my own company,' she countered, elaborately casual. 'Solitude is very different from loneliness. Sometimes it's a blessed relief to get away from other people and their constant demands.' She stopped abruptly, realising she had said far more than she intended. 'Now, perhaps you'll be kind enough to answer my original question and tell me what special circumstances brought you to my doorstep? This is my home, Mr Crossley—' Zanthi's tone was pointed,—'not an extension of Government House.'

'Then, Miss Fitzroy,' his voice was as smooth as cream, 'I must apologise for disturbing you.'

'Oh, you don't *disturb* me,' she retorted sweetly, fiercely glad to see his eyes narrow slightly. 'But I do consider your turning up here something of an intrusion.'

'I take your point.' The blandness of his tone and expression did not fool Zanthi. She felt herself grow tense as she waited for the sting. It came almost at once. 'Though I'm not entirely convinced that standing *outside* your front door qualifies as an intrusion. Still,' he went on, becoming suddenly brisk and giving her no chance to retaliate, 'I will not argue the point.'

Then he smiled. It lit up his whole face, creasing the bronzed skin at the outer corners of his eyes, and deepening the grooves on either side of his mouth. Genuinely warm, and tempered with self-reproach, it caused her heart to leap into her throat then flutter wildly. 'I have a confession to make. It was sheer nervousness that brought me here.'

Zanthi stared at him. 'Oh, yes?' she said at last, openly sceptical.

'You don't believe me?'

'What on earth makes you think that?' she responded drily, her heartbeat uneven.

He shrugged. 'I don't blame you. In your shoes I'd feel exactly the same. The fact remains, I don't like crowds. On a one-to-one basis I'm fine—'

'I'd never have guessed,' murmured Zanthi.

'As I was saying,' he chided, 'attending official functions is one aspect of my job I don't particularly enjoy.'

'Now, isn't that a coincidence?' Zanthi deliberately widened her eyes. 'I feel exactly the same.' She didn't know if he was serious or whether it was yet another attempt to unsettle her. Well, this time she was ready for him. He would get the truth, and if he didn't like it, hard luck.

A little voice warned her that she was not behaving in the best traditions of the

38

Diplomatic Service. Too *bad.* He wasn't sticking to the rules either, and he had started it. 'Being forced to make polite conversation to people with whom one has absolutely nothing in common can be awfully tiring.' She waited, expecting him to recognise the barb and explode.

He merely nodded in agreement. 'I don't know about you, but I find the real killer is trying to connect names and occupations to the right faces. Especially when I've been introduced to twenty different people in the space of an hour.'

Zanthi studied him warily. 'Surely you're sent that kind of information in advance?'

'Normally, yes. But this job came up at very short notice. In fact, I came straight here from Indonesia. So,' he shrugged, 'I'm going in cold.' He spread his hands, palms up, in a gesture of supplication. 'I had hoped—still hope—that despite our rather shaky start, for which I apologise, you might fill me in on whom I'll be meeting tonight, what their political leanings are, and whether they have any financial interest in the scheme.'

A small frown drew Zanthi's brows together. 'Why do you want to know details like that? Surely you'll have enough to remember with just names and occupations?'

'For two reasons.' He stopped. 'Look, do you think I might step *inside* the door? This is a confidential matter, and discussing the people concerned where any passing stranger might overhear is hardly wise. I'm sure you agree?' Even as he spoke he was moving forward.

Caught unawares, her response automatic, Zanthi took a step back, opening the door wider. Then he was over the threshold and inside, without her quite knowing how it had happened.

'Shall I?' The handle was drawn gently but firmly from her grasp and he closed the door. Suddenly the hall seemed tiny and airless. 'That's better. Right, where were we? Oh, yes, the two reasons.'

Zanthi could feel her cheeks burning. She was furious at his unspoken insinuation that she lacked both good manners and any sense of professional security.

Then apprehension ran an icy finger down her spine at the ease with which he, a total stranger, had managed to gain entry to her home, *with her acquiescence.*

'Just a moment,' she found herself saying. 'Do you have some identification?'

The arch of his left brow became more pronounced. 'Naturally. What would you like to see?' He reached into the inside breast-pocket of his dinner jacket. 'My passport? Driving licence?' He thrust both into her hands, then took out a folded sheet of cream paper. 'And this is the letter from the ODA asking me to come out here.'

Zanthi glanced at all three, feeling slightly foolish but none the less determined to do what she knew she should have done the moment she answered the door.

'Happier now?'

Zanthi nodded, looking up as she handed back the documents. She was startled to see that instead of the cool mockery she had expected and, in a way, deserved, his smile was gentle and understanding. 'We are on the same side, you know.'

'You could have fooled me,' Zanthi murmured, recalling his earlier remarks.

'The two reasons?' he reminded her. 'One, background information helps me to fix who's who in my mind.'

'And the other?' Zanthi enquired expressionlessly.

'As I'm sure you're already aware, a scheme of this size will generate cut-throat competition for contracts. When the ODA is involved in a development scheme, they like to know what's *really* going on behind the press releases and official progress reports. Being on the spot I can pass on this information.'

Zanthi stared at him. 'Are you some sort of industrial spy?' There was a hint of awe in her curiosity.

His dark head tipped back and rich laughter bounced off the walls. 'What a wonderfully vivid imagination you have, Miss Fitzroy. No, nothing so glamorous, I'm afraid. I'm simply

41

an impartial observer with a job of my own to do. Speaking of which, no doubt you have a list of the guests attending tonight's dinner. Perhaps we could go through it together now?' Though he phrased it as a request, Zanthi sensed it was an order, one with which he knew she had to comply.

She moved past him, eyes averted, trying to convey a business-like coolness which was surprisingly difficult to maintain. 'You'd better come through.' She led the way into the living-room, aware of his tall frame close behind her, her mouth dry with a nervousness she didn't understand. He had said himself this was a business discussion, and heaven knew she had had plenty of those with visiting diplomats, military personnel, and politicians. All of them had been male, many were pleasant, and a few even attractive. But none had affected her like Garran Crossley, and none had ever come, with or without an invitation, to her home.

That was the problem. He had invaded her territory and in doing so brought the situation to a personal level. She was not able to respond with the same detachment she could have shown had he come to her office in Government House.

Was that why he'd done it? But why should he? What purpose would it serve? She was over-reacting. No one had affected her this way since Jeremy. And she had no intention of treading that path again.

42

Garran Crossley was tremendously attractive. A powerful personality and immensely strong will meant that to get his own way he rarely had even to raise his voice.

Had he been like Paul, vain, glib, a user of people, there wouldn't have been any problem. She would have escorted him as she had a dozen others and, at the end of the evening, she would have consigned his memory to the cabinet along with the files. But he was unlike anyone she had ever met and she felt as though she were trying to run through quicksand.

'What a lovely room,' he said. As she turned he passed her and went to the patio door. 'And that is an amazing view. I hadn't realised how high you were up here.' He glanced at her over his shoulder, indicating the catch. 'May I?'

Zanthi shrugged lightly. 'Please feel free.'

If he noticed the hint of irony he ignored it. Sliding the doors open, he walked out on to the patio and she saw him draw in a deep breath. The sun had almost gone and the sky was washed with pink and lilac. The sea was gun-metal grey and a bank of purple cloud formed a thick line along the horizon.

Turning to face her, he spread his arms, resting his hands on the painted balcony rail. His gaze swept from the mass of blossom on the dividing wall, across the façade of the building and back to linger on Zanthi. 'Beautiful,' he said softly. 'Quite beautiful.'

Her throat grew even drier. 'I've only been here a few weeks,' she found herself saying. 'I had a place in the centre of town before, but it was so noisy—' Already sounding husky, her voice would disappear altogether if she didn't have something to cool and lubricate her throat soon. 'Would you like a drink?'

'That's very kind of you.'

He didn't have to sound so surprised, Zanthi thought venomously. Then she remembered. There wasn't a drop of alcohol in the apartment except for a bottle of white wine she had won in a raffle at a charity auction. 'I—I'm afraid I don't have—'

'I'll have whatever you're having,' he broke in gently, 'as long as it's cold.'

'You don't know what I'm having—' she countered, grateful for his tact and at the same time obscurely angry.

He grinned and shrugged. 'Life's an adventure. I know we got off to a bad start, but you're not likely to try and poison me while I'm a guest in your apartment. It would look just a touch suspicious.' His eyes gleamed with laughter and Zanthi realised he was deliberately teasing her.

Suddenly she didn't want to fight any more, not tonight; she was too tired. Besides, if he really was trying to make amends, it would be ungracious not to make some allowance for his earlier behaviour. He'd just had a long flight and was probably suffering from jet-lag.

44

'Right,' she announced, darting him a smile as she turned towards the kitchen. 'Two Carib Creams coming up!'

'You should do it more often.' His voice came, warm and intimate, from just above and behind her left ear. Her heart gave a lurch then hammered against her ribs as she realised he had followed her. She hadn't expected that. She wished he had stayed on the balcony and given her a few moments' privacy to adjust to yet another change in their brief, erratic acquaintance.

'D-do what?' she stammered, thanking heaven that it had been one of Sarah's days to clean the apartment, then immediately furious with herself for allowing such a thought to cross her mind. She opened the fridge.

She didn't have to impress him. This was *her* apartment, and if it looked like a pigsty, that was no one else's business but hers.

'Smile,' he replied. 'You glow when you smile.'

She straightened up, her hands full, her cheeks on fire. Was that deliberate too? Did he get a kick out of making her blush? She was being ridiculous. He had simply paid her a compliment. True, it wasn't something that happened often—Paul's glib flattery didn't count—but that was no reason to get paranoid.

With hands that were not altogether steady she cut a lemon in half and squeezed the juice into a blender, added milk, a peeled banana

45

and some ice cubes. She glanced up at him. 'There hasn't been a lot to smile about just recently. Could you pass me two tall glasses? They're in the cupboard behind you.'

While he did as she asked, Zanthi switched on the blender.

'I gather you are decidedly overworked at the moment,' he said, setting the glasses down in front of her.

Startled, Zanthi's hand jerked, spilling the liquid down the outside of one glass. 'Damn!' she muttered. He passed her the dishcloth. 'And just how did you manage to gather that?' she demanded, her cool, noncommittal tone belied by the tremor in hands that threatened to spill more of the creamy slush as she filled the two glasses.

'I was introduced to Lieutenant Benham this afternoon,' came the cryptic reply. 'I've met a lot of people like him in the course of my work.' Cynicism edged his voice.

Zanthi went to the sink and rinsed the cloth. She was terrified he would say more, forcing her, out of professional loyalty, to defend Paul. But again, as if reading her thoughts, he stopped.

She kept her back to him, twisting the cloth tighter and tighter. 'D-did he suggest you came here?' She didn't want to ask but she had to know.

'Good God, no.'

The astonishment in Garran Crossley's

voice was genuine and Zanthi was surprised by the strength of her relief.

'It's hardly likely he would do that.'

Zanthi hung the cloth over the cold tap and turned round. 'Oh?' She kept her face expressionless.

'Well, professionally speaking, he has no right to send or invite anyone to your apartment—'

'That didn't stop you coming,' Zanthi interrupted.

'Ah, but that was my idea, no one else's,' he replied at once. 'I also got the impression that there is something between you?' The slight upward inflection turned his remark into a question.

'A totally mistaken impression,' Zanthi stated flatly. How *dared* Paul do such a thing! *If he did*, a small voice pointed out. Or could it be that Garran Crossley was just fishing?

'I see.' There was a gleam in his eye which Zanthi could not interpret. It made her uneasy.

'I don't think you do,' she retorted, 'but it doesn't matter.' She passed him one of the glasses.

He raised it, his gaze bold and full of laughter. 'Here's to a pleasant evening.'

Lips twitching in spite of herself, Zanthi lifted her own glass in silent, ironic salute, and drank. The creamy, ice-cold liquid slid down her throat like soothing nectar.

He looked at his glass. 'That's rather nice.'

'You sound surprised,' Zanthi's tone was dry.

'I must admit it's not an aperitif I'm familiar with.'

'Then you haven't lived,' she retorted lightly.

His eyelids lowered a fraction, giving him the deceptively lazy look of a predator, and Zanthi's nerves vibrated: 'So I'm beginning to realise. Tell me, do you have any more recipes for milkshakes?'

Zanthi went pink but managed to keep her voice light. He'd pay for that. 'Yes, several, actually. But Caleb, the barman at Government House, makes a fruit cup I think you'll find more to your taste.'

'I'll be sure to try it. Now, let's go and sit down.'

Zanthi stiffened. 'What for?' The words were out before she could stop them and she cringed. How gauche she sounded, like a nervous schoolgirl.

'You were going to tell me about the people I have to meet tonight,' he reminded her gently.

Zanthi bent her head, staring blindly, into her glass. He must think her a complete fool and who could blame him? The pressures of the past few weeks had obviously affected her more deeply than she realised for her nerves to be in this state.

'Of course,' she tried to smile but her cheeks felt stiff. 'I'm sorry I—'

He covered her mouth lightly with his fingertips and, as their eyes met and locked, slowly shook his head.

They were both utterly still. Zanthi forgot to breathe. The apartment seemed to recede and there was nothing left in the world but his eyes and the warmth of his touch on her lips. The moment was shattered by the sharp, insistent trill of the telephone.

CHAPTER THREE

As Zanthi stumbled into the hall and lifted the receiver, she was trembling from head to foot. 'Hello?' she croaked. Closing her eyes, and leaning back against the wall, she dragged air deep into her lungs. She *had* to pull herself together. But that was easier said than done. Though the man was a total stranger, that silencing gesture had been more intimate than any kiss she had received in the last three years.

Margaret's voice, high-pitched and agitated, came down the line. 'Zanthi? I'm sorry, I know you've got company, but can you come back right away? I would have asked Lieutenant Benham but he'd only make things worse and anyway I can't find him, though it doesn't take a lot of imagination to guess where—'

'Just a second, Margaret,' Zanthi interrupted the flow, pressing her fingers to her forehead. What had she said? *I know you've got company. How* did she know? Unless—so that was how he had got her address. What yarn had he spun Margaret? It must have been a good one . . . That would have to wait. Right now she had to find out what had pushed Margaret to the verge of hysterics. 'Now,' she soothed, marvelling at how calm her voice sounded while her mind resembled a spin-dryer on high speed, 'tell me what's wrong.'

Garran Crossley appeared in the sitting-room doorway and Zanthi shot upright as if she'd been stung. He was still holding his glass which now contained only an inch of the Carib Cream. Leaning one immaculately clad shoulder against the jamb, he raised the glass to his lips and drained the remainder.

Zanthi's eyes were drawn to the strong muscles in his neck which moved as he swallowed. Then she realised he had not shifted his gaze. *He was watching her watching him.*

Her cheeks on fire, she half-turned away, pressing the receiver hard against her ear. But Margaret was in such a state she was almost shouting and Zanthi winced at the assault on her eardrum.

'Hyacinth is what's wrong,' Margaret

50

shrilled. 'You know that medicine she takes for her throat? Well, she's been at it all day, straight from the bottle, according to Millie.' A cold weight settled on Zanthi's stomach. 'Millie won't say exactly what happened, but Hyacinth is raving and Caleb has locked himself in the pantry and refuses to come out.'

Zanthi glanced swiftly sideways and caught Garran's eye. His dark brows were raised in an expression of mute amazement and enquiry. He had obviously heard every word.

She turned her back on him. Couldn't he see this was a private matter? Had he no tact? Clapping her hand over the receiver, she forced herself to smile as she looked over her shoulder at him. 'I'm awfully sorry, this won't take a moment. Perhaps you'd like another look at the view from the balcony?'

'That's very thoughtful of you.' The bland smile that tilted the corners of his mouth bore no relation to the laughter that glistened in his brown eyes. 'But, to be honest, it doesn't hold a candle to the view right here.'

'*Zanthi? Are you still there?*' Margaret's muffled squawk issued from the receiver and Zanthi raised it to her ear once more, holding it tightly in both hands as she tried to marshal her thoughts. The practical aspects were her first priority.

'Had Hyacinth finished preparing the meal before . . .' Zanthi crossed her fingers in fervent hope, heedless of Garran's quizzical

51

gaze.

'I think so, there were pans bubbling on the stove and there seemed to be a lot of stuff laid out in the cold room. To be honest, I didn't stay long enough to check. I thought I'd better get hold of you first.'

'You did exactly right,' Zanthi reassured her. 'I'm glad you didn't reach the ADC. This is a domestic matter involving staff, and so it's my responsibility. Did you manage to talk to Hyacinth? I know she's not the easiest—'

'Talk to her?' Margaret shrieked. 'She's in no mood to talk to anyone. I told you, she's raving. When I left the kitchen she was hammering on the pantry door, clutching one of those huge knives. She was shouting, Caleb was shouting, it's uproar, Zanthi.'

'Oh, my God,' Zanthi whispered, leaning weakly, against the wall. There were thirty people arriving for dinner in less than an hour. 'Where are the rest of the kitchen staff?'

'Dennis has mustered them in the toolshed and is organising what he calls a tactical force to free Caleb.'

'Oh, no.' Zanthi's face mirrored her horror and she jerked upright. 'I'm on my way, Margaret. For heaven's sake try to keep Dennis out until I get there.' She slammed the phone down. Garran was already passing her on his way to the front door.

'You fetch your bag and lock up, I'll get a taxi,' he announced and disappeared, his brisk

52

footsteps receding down the tiled outer hall.

Zanthi clung to the strap in a desperate effort to stop herself being hurled against him a second time as the cab swayed and jolted over the rough road. The driver was crooning a reggae number, beating out the rhythm on the steering wheel.

She knew she was still flushed. She could feel it. Not just in her face but in the heat of her body. The tepid shower barely an hour ago had been a complete waste of time. She was hot and sticky and doubtless her nose was shining like a traffic-light.

When the cornering cab flung her across his lap, he made no effort to hold her, but neither did he help her up. She didn't know whether to apologise or simply ignore what had happened. His glimpsed expression, a strange mixture of amusement, reflectiveness and cynicism, only deepened her confusion.

She could still feel the hard, sinewy length of his thigh and the solid warmth of his chest beneath the crisp dress-shirt. The fragrance of his cologne still lingered in her nostrils, faint but tantalising. Zanthi loosened the high neck of her dress and turned her flushed face to the slightly open window, hoping desperately for a cooling breeze.

'This throat medicine your cook appears to rely on,' he began, and immediately Zanthi knew from his tone that he had guessed the truth.

53

She glanced briefly at him, pulling a wry face. 'Gin,' she said succinctly.

He nodded. 'I thought as much. I take it Margaret doesn't know?'

Zanthi shook her head and sighed. 'I haven't the heart to tell her. She and Hyacinth are about the same age and usually get on well. Hyacinth doesn't go over the top very often,' she added quickly.

'Shame it wasn't rum,' Garran mused. 'Gin is such a depressive, especially for women. Is she a good cook?'

Zanthi, who had been staring at him, started. 'Marvellous. And she's incredibly versatile. She can produce English, French or Creole dishes from the same ingredients just by altering the spices and sauces. It's just that now and again—' Zanthi gestured helplessly and raked one hand through her hair. 'Why tonight of all nights?' she groaned.

'Don't worry on my account.' He touched her hand lightly and the caress set her nerves quivering so that the imprint of his fingertips. lingered long after the pressure had gone. 'Travelling as much as I do, and mostly to out-of-the-way places, I've developed a cast-iron stomach.'

'Actually, I wasn't thinking of you,' she replied, which at that moment happened to be the truth. Then, realising how curt she had sounded, Zanthi went a deeper shade of pink. She reached over and closed the glass partition between them and the driver. 'You see, the smooth running of the domestic side of Government House is my responsibility. I do the hiring and firing, so any problems relating to staff land on my desk.'

'You seem to carry a great deal of responsibility for—'

'A woman?' she supplied tartly.

'I was going to say, for one so young,' he responded. 'But in either case you seem perfectly capable of handling it.'

She darted him a wry, apologetic smile. 'I could have done without this little lot.'

'Enough on your plate already?' he sympathised.

'You could say that. I don't know, things never happen one at a time when you can deal with them in order. It seems to be all or nothing.'

'And you're not getting the support you're entitled to?'

Zanthi sighed. It was strange. For someone who had the power to affect her so deeply, he was surprisingly easy to talk to. 'It's not the actual work so much. Margaret is wonderful. She relieves me of a lot of the basic routine. It's—I don't know, I just have the feeling—like there's gas leaking and it's building up for an explosion, but no one can smell it except me.'

'And you've tried talking about it but no one will listen,' he said quietly.

She nodded. 'Paul thinks I'm making

55

mountains out of molehills. He says all the demonstrations are just democracy in action. Anyway, he's more interested in his own concerns right now.'

'And the Governor?' There was almost no curiosity in his tone. He gave the impression of not really caring whether she answered or not, of only making polite conversation.

'He's only interested in his garden,' she retorted. 'I don't think he's aware of what's going on in the island half the time.' She stopped, the blood draining from her face, horrified at this totally uncharacteristic lack of discretion. Whatever had come over her? How could she be talking this way to someone she barely knew?

He nodded absently then, turning back from the window, frowned. 'What about this chap who's locked himself in the pantry? Why does Hyacinth want to kill him?'

In spite of her anxiety and the horror which had momentarily chilled her, Zanthi couldn't help smiling. 'Killing Caleb is the very last thing Hyacinth has in mind.'

Garran's left brow rose, but he remained silent, waiting for Zanthi to explain.

'If you're thinking about the knife, don't,' she said. 'Hyacinth probably isn't even aware she's holding it, and she certainly wouldn't use it on Caleb *deliberately*.'

'Really?' Garran's tone was dry. 'I'm sure if I were in Caleb's place I'd find that immensely comforting.'

'When Hyacinth is sober,' Zanthi explained, 'she's a model of moral virtue, a pillar of the church, and a thoroughly respectable single lady. It's just that, now and again . . . I can usually see it coming when she starts complaining about her throat. I suppose I've been too busy lately. I didn't realise . . .'

'Do I take it Hyacinth is suffering from a severe case of unrequited love?' he suggested.

Zanthi's head jerked round. *He had a mind like a scalpel.* She nodded. 'I'm afraid so. Caleb is thirty. He married his childhood sweetheart and they have four children. He's a quiet, rather shy man, a good listener rather than a talker. Which is one of the reasons, apart from knowing every cocktail yet created, he's so popular with the guests at Government House, especially the regulars.'

'And the pious, lusty Miss Hyacinth scares the pants off him,' Garran mused.

Zanthi started to giggle. She tried to stifle it, but found she couldn't. Everything was falling apart around her and now she was going to pieces too. Dimly she recognised she was reacting to the emotional hammering she had undergone recently, but that didn't help.

'I'm glad you're getting some enjoyment out of all this.' The deep voice was cool.

She stopped laughing at once. 'Is that—what you think?' Her eyes were over-bright, her face pinched with strain. 'Let me assure

57

you, Mr Crossley, *enjoyment* is the last thing on my mind right now. With all I've got to cope with, Hyacinth's emotional problems are something I could happily have done without. But, of course, working alone with no one but yourself to consider, you wouldn't understand what I'm talking about.'

His gaze, as it met hers, was unreadable, but Zanthi had the uneasy feeling that once again he had somehow provoked her into saying far more than she would normally have done.

'Leaving aside your opinions of me and my work for the moment, I *still* don't know a damn thing about anyone I'm meeting tonight.'

Zanthi's hand flew to her mouth. 'Oh. I'm so sorry. I'd forgotten all about . . .'

'Which is understandable in the circumstances,' he broke in. 'But now, do you think, just a thumbnail sketch?'

Zanthi's cast another glance at the closed glass partition, then closed her eyes, focusing her attention on visualising various members of the Assembly.

'Is there a tradesmen's entrance?' he cut in as they approached the main gate.

Zanthi nodded. 'At the back. But there isn't a separate drive.' She frowned in concern. 'We're going to took awfully conspicuous sailing straight past the front door.'

Garran grinned. 'Then we'll just have to take the scenic route. Stop here,' he instructed the driver, who glanced round, shrugged, and pulled up a few yards short of the main gate with its ceremonial guard of cadets.

After the cab had roared away in a cloud of blue exhaust fumes, the driver still crooning, there was a short delay while the elder of the two cadets, snapping smartly to attention, asked to see their invitations.

'For heaven's sake, George,' Zanthi said with barely contained impatience, 'I work here, as you very well know. And Mr Crossley is one of the Governor's guests.'

'Then he'll have an invitation, miss,' the youth pointed out, his back ramrod-straight, his face brick-red.

'Just following orders, miss.' His companion's tone held a note of pleading.

'You're a credit to your instructor,' Garran said smoothly and reached into his inside pocket. 'I'm afraid I don't have an invitation card. I'm a substitute, you see. The chap who has the card is ill, and I've come along in his place. As he's in England and I've come from Indonesia, he wasn't able to pass it on.' He took out his passport and driver's licence and offered them to the boy, who looked faintly nonplussed. 'Will these do as proof of my identity? You can check with Lieutenant Benham if you wish.'

Clearly wishing he'd kept quiet, the youth gave the documents a cursory glance and handed them back. 'No, sir. That's fine. Thank you, sir.'

'Don't hurry,' Garran murmured softly to Zanthi as they started up the drive. 'Tell me about the shrubs and flowers.'

Zanthi looked at him sharply. 'Are you out of your mind?' she whispered. 'Have you forgotten—'

'Do it,' he hissed, glancing over his shoulder, 'and use your arms. Point things out.' He nodded as though agreeing with some remark she had just made and indicated a tall coconut palm, turning to look up at it as they walked round the slight curve in the drive. Then she realised that, though his head was tilted back as though he were studying the tree, his eyes were darting between the entrance to the house, where two more, cadets were directing guests into the reception rooms, and the gate where a large black limousine had just drawn up.

'Right.' His fingers fastened around her arm just above the elbow. 'Now.' An instant later they were off the drive and hidden in the cool, dark shade of the bushes.

As he guided her swiftly through the shrubbery and round to the back of the house, Zanthi's heart quickened and a tiny flicker of excitement twisted inside her.

'How very cloak-and-dagger,' she whispered, slightly breathless, wondering what state her pale shoes would be in after this dash across the damp earth. 'Do you do this sort of thing often?'

He looked down at her. 'All the time,' he replied, straight-faced.

They emerged from the shrubbery into the vegetable garden just as Dennis and his small bunch of followers reached the back door.

'*Damn!*' Garran muttered, then, raising his voice, called, 'Sergeant!'

Dennis whirled round, clearly furious. The kitchen staff looked relieved, their faces breaking into uncertain smiles as they saw Zanthi.

'There's been a change of plan.' Garran's voice was low-pitched but carried clearly as he strode forward. 'Your rescue idea was a brilliant piece of strategy, but the Governor dares not risk it.'

Dennis's small eyes widened and his mouth dropped momentarily. 'The Governor knows?' he whispered.

'He's anxious to keep the whole incident under wraps,' Garran replied, his tone hushed and serious. 'He needs you at the front entrance. Your job is to allay suspicion. British prestige is at stake here. No one must suspect there is anything wrong. That won't be easy, knowing what you do, but the success of the entire evening is in your hands and this dinner has a bearing on the island's future.'

Dennis seemed stunned for a moment.

'Can you handle it?' Garran demanded.

Dennis's chest swelled visibly. 'Just you leave it to me.' He tucked his chin in and set his cap more squarely on his bullet-shaped head. Then concern battled with pride and determination. 'But what about Caleb, sir? We can't just leave him in there with that madwoman?'

'He's quite safe at the moment, locked in the pantry.'

Zanthi stared at Garran. There was not the slightest trace of levity in his voice or expression. His whole manner towards Dennis was one of utter seriousness and total sincerity.

'The Governor feels,' he went on, 'that this is a case of diplomacy rather than a show of strength.' He lowered his voice conspiratorially. 'A woman's touch, you understand?'

Dennis sucked his teeth and looked worried. 'Miss Blaine and Millie don't seem to be having much success.'

'They haven't the benefit of Miss Fitzroy's diplomatic training,', Garran pointed out. 'Her handling of emotional situations is quite unique, believe me.' He caught Zanthi's eye for a split second and to her intense annoyance she felt her colour rise.

'Is that so, sir?' Dennis sounded impressed and Zanthi felt like hitting them both.

'Besides,' Garran pointed out, 'I'll be there to back her up; just in case. The most important thing is that the whole business remains top secret. The Governor's reputation for running a tight ship could be at stake.'

'Right, sir.' Dennis snapped a stiff salute. 'I'll get on to it at once. Can't have anyone pointing the finger at His Excellency.'

'Good man.' Garran clapped him on the shoulder. 'I knew we could depend on you.' Dennis marched swiftly away, expression intent, his boots crunching importantly on the gravel as Garran turned to the kitchen staff. 'Just wait here a moment.' He beckoned Zanthi forward. 'Shall we go?'

She shook her head as she passed him. 'It's a pity you aren't in films,' she hissed. 'That performance would have won you an Oscar.'

He looked hurt. 'I meant every word.'

Openly sceptical, Zanthi tilted her head sideways. 'All that stuff about the Governor wants and the Governor feels—'

'Just supposing he *did* know,' Garran broke in softly, 'do you think he would have reacted differently?'

Would he have reacted at all? Zanthi wondered and immediately felt ashamed. That was disloyal. 'N—no, probably not,' she admitted.

'Well, then?' The noise got louder as they went down the passage. Garran pushed open the swing door into the kitchen and the heat and racket hit Zanthi like a wall.

Millie was shouting as she juggled pans on the vast stove. Margaret was trying to placate her and at the same time to calm Hyacinth, whose white-overalled bulk overflowed a chair drawn up to the scrubbed wooden table.

Clutching a large, brown medicine bottle in one plump hand and the knife in the other, Hyacinth only paused in her wailing long enough to shriek her grievances at the pantry-door.

'You're not going to be able to talk her out of it, she's too far gone to reason with,' Garran said as he watched her sway back and forward, sobbing noisily.

Margaret's eyes rolled heavenward in an expression of helplessness as she patted the heaving shoulders. She made a move towards the medicine bottle, but Hyacinth snatched it out of reach and, after hugging it to her huge bosom for a moment raised it to her lips.

'Thank you, Mr Crossley,' Zanthi said with saccharine sweetness. 'I had actually reached that conclusion on my own, but it's always useful to have an expert opinion.' She beckoned Millie towards her. 'I don't want to know where you get it from or who it belongs to, but find me some jack-iron. Half a cupful should be enough. And Millie, be as quick as you can, the guests are arriving.'

Her eyes enormous, the skinny girl nodded swiftly and, thrusting the wooden spoon into Zanthi's hand, darted out of the kitchen.

'What are you going to do?' Garran asked as she checked the contents of various pans.

'To paraphrase something someone said to me quite recently, desperate circumstances call

64

for desperate measures.' Zanthi hoped fervently that she sounded more confident than she felt.

The door burst open and Millie dashed in clutching a clear bottle, half-full of dark, treacly-looking liquid. 'You want some blackcurrant cordial to go with this?' she panted.

'Millie, you're a genius,' Zanthi said over her shoulder as she reached for a mug and poured out a generous measure of the local quick-kick rum. Topping it up with the cordial, she stirred the mixture with the handle of the wooden spoon then, carrying it across to the cook, laid a comforting hand on her shoulder. 'Hyacinth, you drink this up. It will take all the hurt and pain away . . .'

'You are quite a resourceful lady,' Garran remarked as they crossed the lawns in front of the shrubbery ten minutes later and hurried round to the front of the house.

Zanthi moved her shoulders awkwardly. 'Hyacinth regards the kitchen as her personal domain. She would never have left of her own free will and it was obvious no one could work while she was still there. Knocking her out with the rum was the only answer.' She was quiet for a moment. 'Poor thing, she'll have a dreadful hangover in the morning.'

'Let's hope, for all our sakes, it's accompanied by total amnesia,' Garran said drily.

As they walked up the wide shallow steps to the porticoed entrance, past two more cadets, Zanthi saw Paul striding towards them, dazzling in his white full-dress uniform. He radiated resentment and curiosity and she sighed.

Garran's hand cupped her elbow and gave it a reassuring squeeze as Paul bore down on them, almost strutting with self-importance.

'Good evening,' Mr Crossley.' His smile was a mere rictus of facial muscles.

Instant antipathy, thought Zanthi, she should have expected it.

As Paul's gaze flicked to her, his petulant mouth thinned and his blue eyes grew small in his sunburnt face. 'You're late.'

Embarrassment and anger bloomed like twin roses on Zanthi's cheeks.

Instantly, Garran's fingers tightened on her elbow and before she could draw breath to reply, he cut in. '*If* Miss Fitzroy is late, Lieutenant Benham,' he said pleasantly, 'the fault is entirely mine. Her knowledge of the island is of vital importance to my work here and, not having had time this afternoon, I wanted the chance to speak to her before meeting the rest of this evening's guests. I naturally assumed that, being my assigned escort, she would be giving me her undivided attention. However—' He allowed the word to hang, suspended in the silence.

Zanthi froze. *Oh, God, he wasn't going to*

66

mention Hyacinth, was he? That really would put the cat among the pigeons, *and* give Paul more ammunition with which to snipe at her.

'If for some pressing reason you need Miss Fitzroy,' Garran continued, 'I'm sure if I explain the problem to the Governor he will—'

'No,' Paul blurted, his smile glassy. 'No, I was simply concerned on your account. Women do have this tendency to forget the time.' He laughed, showing all his teeth and Zanthi felt an overpowering urge to kick him.

As Garran glanced down at her, she saw the laughter in his eyes and realised he knew exactly what she was thinking. 'How kind,' he said blandly, 'but your concern is quite unnecessary.' One corner of his mouth flickered. 'Miss Fitzroy suits me perfectly.'

As Paul's mouth thinned almost to invisibility, Zanthi felt herself propelled forward past him and realised Garran Crossley had deliberately phrased his remark to allow for more than one interpretation. Her heart gave an odd flutter, but the sensation was lost as her temper began to rise. Just what was going on? She had no intention of being a pawn in any power struggle. It was only too obvious which of the two men would win. Besides, as she was Paul's deputy, her loyalty *had* to be to him, regardless of her personal feelings.

'Smile,' Garran murmured, his breath warm against her ear. 'Relax. This is supposed to be

67

a pleasant social occasion.'

Zanthi dug her heels in, forcing him to stop just outside the doorway of a high-ceilinged reception-room already half-full of people. 'It certainly got off to a brilliant start,' she muttered. 'Look, I don't know what you're up to—'

'Up to?' His dark brows rose.

'Don't play the innocent with me,' she retorted: ' "Miss Fitzroy suits me perfectly." Just don't get any ideas. I'm spending this evening with you because it's my job to do so. I wasn't given any choice. Last week I escorted the captain of a visiting warship. Next week it will be someone else.'

'My, what a busy life you do lead.' He smiled down at her. 'And did *they* have to smuggle you into the grounds and watch you administer a knock-out dose of alcohol to a hysterical cook so that you could rescue the bartender who had locked himself up to protect his virtue? Is that a regular part of the evening's entertainment at Government House?'

'No,' Zanthi responded tartly. 'You were privileged.'

Light flared in his eyes and she knew she had jolted him. It had not been intentional. There was just something about him which, every so often, made her want to lash out to keep him at a distance.

He laughed, a soft sound that came from

68

deep in his chest. It curled around Zanthi's heart and she had difficulty breathing.

'Then you owe me, Miss Fitzroy.' His voice was low and unexpectedly husky. 'And you can be sure that, one way or another, I intend to collect.'

Zanthi's eyes widened. She felt the colour drain momentarily from her face only to flood back in a hot, engulfing tide.

She had to get away even if it was only for a few minutes. Her heart was pounding furiously and her legs felt like soft rubber. It was ridiculous that he should affect her this way. She was used to dealing with awkward people and difficult situations. But he was something else again and nothing that had gone before had prepared her for Garran Crossley's uncanny ability to bypass her protective shell as though it simply did not exist. The more she saw of him the more vulnerable he made her feel, and that worried her.

She snatched at the sleeve of an elderly man who was passing. 'Good evening, Minister.' Her voice was hoarse, her throat dry and tense with nerves. 'May I present Mr Garran Crossley, the land surveyor who will be giving us the benefit of his knowledge and experience in building roads across hostile terrain?'

The Minister's jowly face broke into a delighted smile and as the two men shook hands Zanthi made her escape, but not before Garran had shot her a look which threatened

69

reprisal for her defection.

When Zanthi returned five minutes later she felt refreshed and much calmer. She had repaired her make-up, run cold water over her wrists, and convinced herself her fears were simply the product of tension and an over-active imagination. Pausing for a moment in the doorway, she looked briefly around the elegant room. Light from the chandeliers was reflected off the medals of the retired officers acting as honorary ADCs. The black dinner jackets of the other male guests provided the perfect contrast to their ladies' dresses, the colours of which ranged from pastel to primary. Lilac, pink and misty blue mingled with emerald, buttercup and crimson.

The rumble of conversation and occasional burst of laughter had risen in volume as acquaintance was renewed and gossip passed on, eased by a steady flow of alcohol dispensed with swift efficiency by Caleb, who showed no visible signs of his recent ordeal.

Some people stood about in groups, spilling out through the French doors which opened on to the garden, while others sat on brocade-covered sofas. Behind them hidden lights illuminated delicate ornaments and fine glass displayed in alcoves. The cream walls, white paintwork and jade-green curtains created an atmosphere of cool, elegant spaciousness, and to Zanthi's surprise and relief the air-conditioning seemed to be working. On side-tables and pedestals, floral arrangements of cream and bronze with touches of lemon and pale orange, framed by fresh green foliage, added their own colour and fragrance to the scene.

Zanthi watched the eddy and swirl of people around the Governor as he and Lady Fiona, with Paul hovering in attendance, progressed on their slow circuit of the room, stopping to speak to each guest or group in turn.

She felt the fine hair on her arms lift and an instant later saw Garran Crossley approaching. Inches taller than anyone else, he threaded his way through the throng towards her, his eyes locked on hers, the expression in them mocking the polite smile that curved his mobile mouth.

'If you do it again I shall be forced to lodge a strong complaint with His Excellency,' he threatened softly.

Cold fingers clawed at her gut and her attempt to remain cool and aloof failed miserably. 'Do what?'

'Disappear and leave me to the not-so-tender mercies of predatory females.' He kept his voice low and the bland smile never faltered. 'I have been propositioned three times already.'

Zanthi stared up at him, not sure whether he was serious. She moistened her lips. 'I'm sure you are perfectly capable of handling that situation. After all, you must be used to it.' As the words left her lips, too late to be recalled, Zanthi wished the floor would open and swallow her. She had no right to say such things. It was unforgivable. *Even if it was true.*

She raised stricken eyes to his. But before she could mumble an apology, he leaned closer.

'That is not the point.' His gaze was hypnotic, demanding, reaching into her very soul. 'I was promised your undivided attention for the entire evening. And that is what I intend to have.'

Zanthi felt a funny, sliding sensation in her stomach and the rest of the evening passed in a blur. It was as though they were connected by an invisible cord. Each time she strayed more than an arm's length from his side, she felt the tug. If she glanced up or round he would be watching her, still maintaining his conversation with someone else.

It brought goose-pimples up on her skin at first. But as the evening wore on she grew used to it.

She introduced him to everyone he was supposed to meet and kept him circulating. When they sat down at the long banqueting-table she answered his questions about the geography of the island and gave him additional information about the people he had met.

She was vaguely aware of the courses

arriving and being cleared away: avocado mousse, consommé Julienne, scallops with a Creole sauce of coconut cream and spices. Then, after a short break decreed by the Governor for a sorbet to clear the palate, the main course was served. It was the Governor's favourite. Fillet of beef Wellington with Madeira sauce, accompanied by roast potatoes; lyonnaise potatoes, golden brown and savoury with onion; baton carrots, buttered sliced courgettes, and french green beans. The meal concluded with a choice of exotic fruit salad or strawberry pavlova, followed by tiny cups of aromatic coffee.

Zanthi forced herself to eat, knowing her nerves needed nourishment if she was to cope with the added and unexpected upheaval of Garran Crossley's intrusion into her life. But the food stuck like so much sawdust in her throat and, in an effort to get it down, she took frequent sips from her wine-glass, not realising it was refilled twice.

By the time the coffee was poured, she was surprised at how pleasantly relaxed she felt. Garran's quiet questioning seemed interested rather than intrusive and she had to admit he took a weight off her by shouldering the burden of making conversation. He kept it light and amusing, relating anecdotes concerning some of the things that had happened to him during the course of his work in various countries.

But when the Governor rose, signifying the end of the meal, and everyone else stood up too, Zanthi swayed and would have fallen back into her chair had Garran not instantly but unobtrusively gripped her elbow. She was bewildered, then amazed, and finally horrified as the awful truth dawned. *She couldn't be.* She'd only had one glass of wine, *one long, endless glass of wine.* Then she heard herself begin to giggle.

'Time to go home,' Garran murmured.

'Not with you,' she retorted at once as the room rocked slowly.

'I can't let you go alone,' he pointed out. 'Apart from the fact that it goes against my upbringing, in your present state anything could happen to you.'

'And who is responsible for my present state?' She stabbed his chest with an accusing finger, blinking owlishly up at him. 'I might be very slightly tipsy,' she enunciated carefully, 'but I'm not stupid. So whatever ideas you have . . .' her cheeks grew even rosier '. . . well, you can just forget them.'

He tutted, shaking his head slowly. 'What an ego. Strange as it may seem to you, Miss Fitzroy, I have never yet had to get a woman drunk in order to make love to her. In fact, I find it hard to imagine anything less erotic or pleasurable. Perhaps you believe otherwise. Lieutenant Benham is coming this way. Shall I ask him to . . . ?'

'*No!*' Zanthi shook her head quickly, her voice a hoarse whisper: 'No, please don't.' The words tumbled out in desperation. 'He's been trying for ages to get an invitation to my flat. I don't want him there. Please?'

Steered sharply away from the ADC who had been momentarily waylaid by the Finance Minister's wife, Zanthi found herself being propelled along the hall and out on to the wide steps. A fleet of cars lined the drive and, seconds later, without quite knowing how, Zanthi was in the back seat of a taxi with Garran's arm resting lightly on her shoulders and her head pillowed on his chest as they swept down the hill.

She was drawn reluctantly from a delicious sensation of floating on a bed of fluffy pink clouds by Garran gently shaking her, his breath warm on her cheeks as he repeated twice, three times, that she was home.

In the limbo between sleep and consciousness she murmured smiling agreement and nestled against his shoulder once more. But he eased her away, out of the car, and on to her feet.

She came round then, blinking like a dishevelled owl in the light from the doorway.

His hand cupping her elbow, he walked her to her door. She fumbled in her purse for her key, then, clutching it in trembling fingers, slowly turned to look at him, her defences breached by the combined effects of weariness, wine, the drama of Hyacinth, and the close collaboration of the past three hours. Driven by an aching loneliness her conscious mind normally refused to acknowledge, she lifted her face in a silent plea to be kissed.

He gazed at her for a long moment, studying her features as though committing them to memory. The passage light was behind him, his face in shadow, making it impossible for her to read the expression in his dark eyes. His mouth tightened, a muscle jumping at the point of his jaw. Then slowly, almost reluctantly, he ran his fingertips down the side of her face and she quivered at his touch.

Taking the key from her, he unlocked the door. Zanthi's heartbeat threatened to choke her as he turned to her once more. But, pressing the key into her hand, he pushed her gently into the flat.

'Goodnight, Zanthi,' he said softly, and, pulling the door closed, he walked away.

She stood immobile until the sound of his receding footsteps had disappeared completely. Then, half-mortified, half-grateful, totally confused, she undressed and fell into bed, expecting to toss and turn and agonise over all that had, and had not happened. Within minutes she was sound asleep.

CHAPTER FOUR

It was mid-afternoon the following day before Zanthi had either time or opportunity to tackle Margaret about revealing her address to Garran Crossley.

'I'm sorry, Zanthi.' Margaret rubbed her hands uneasily, making a dry, rasping sound. 'It just slipped out. He was so pleasant and friendly. He said how beautiful it was here and asked if any of the office staff actually live at Government House. I told him no, well, only the ADC. The rest of us all lived in or around Arlington. He made some sympathetic remarks about the time and inconvenience involved in travelling to and fro, and I said it isn't really a problem as it gives us time to wind down and leave work behind, though it wasn't quite so easy for you as you often had evening functions to attend.'

She raised her shoulders, clearly bemused by her own behaviour. 'He was so interested, Zanthi, but he didn't seem at all curious. Does that make sense? Anyway, I found myself telling him where we all lived and how long it took to get here . . .' She broke off, shaking her head, her face furrowed with concern. 'I didn't even realise I'd done it until he said it was important for him to speak to you before beginning the official business of meeting everyone, and didn't I think the most sensible way of killing two birds with one stone was for him to call and collect you.'

Zanthi's residual irritation was swept away by a wave of understanding and sympathy. How could she be angry with Margaret? Hadn't Garran Crossley had exactly the same effect on her? Hadn't she found herself responding to his apparently innocuous questions, only realising *afterwards* just how much she had told him?

'I am sorry, Zanthi.' Margaret's expression grew faintly alarmed. 'He wasn't any trouble, was he? I mean, he didn't . . .' she went pink, '. . . he wasn't a nuisance?' The mixture of distaste and embarrassment with which she invested the word almost made Zanthi smile.

But a vivid memory of Garran Crossley's fingertips resting lightly on her lips made her tingle from head to foot as though an electric current had passed through her. 'No.' She shook her head briefly, lashes veiling her eyes as she struggled to keep sudden confusion out of her face and voice. 'In fact, all things considered, it's a good job he was with me when you rang. Heaven knows, I've learnt to think on my feet, but I couldn't have handled Dennis the way he did.' There was grudging admiration in her tone. 'Can you imagine what might have happened if Dennis had actually launched his rescue bid and stormed the kitchen?' She shuddered.

78

'*Don't*.' Margaret raised her hands, fending off the all-too-vivid picture. 'It doesn't bear thinking about.'

Zanthi passed her a pile of files. 'Has Hyacinth come in today?'

Margaret nodded, clasping the folders to her polyester-frilled bosom. 'About an hour ago. But as there was no official lunch today, Millie had already prepared cold cuts, mixed salads and fruit tarts.'

'Millie deserves a rise as well as a medal,' Zanthi decided.

'I haven't seen Hyacinth myself,' Margaret continued, 'but when I rang down, Millie said that apart from looking as pale and fragile as it's possible for someone of her size and colour to look, Hyacinth seemed to be back to normal.'

'Thank God for that.' Zanthi darted a look at her secretary. 'Does she remember anything?' She grimaced. 'Like who's to blame for her splitting headache and scoured stomach?'

Margaret shrugged. 'We're not sure. According to Millie, Hyacinth is doing an excellent impression of a zip-fastener. She's not talking to anybody. However, she *is* singing all her favourite hymns with a sort of quiet desperation. Millie thinks Hyacinth does have a hazy recollection of what happened, but can't bear to think about it, and accepts how she's feeling as her punishment.'

79

Zanthi knew a moment's intense compassion for the cook, whose infatuation for Caleb was in violent conflict with her strong religious principles. She offered up a swift mental prayer of thanks that she was free of all that. Since Jeremy, she had thrown herself into work, kept mind and body fully occupied, and been grateful for the numbness that smothered her emotions, allowing the painful wounds time to heal. Apart from a few surface ripples and an occasional grieving for something she had never known, she had been comfortably distanced from the mouth-drying, earth-shifting feelings tearing at Hyacinth. Until yesterday.

Margaret leaned forward, glancing over her shoulder in an instinctive check to ensure they were entirely alone. 'I didn't suppose I should say this, and I know it's none of my business, but I have a suspicion that medicine Hyacinth is taking for her throat—' Margaret lowered her voice to a whisper—'I think it contains *alcohol.*'

Margaret had never been known to take more than one glass of sweet sherry in an entire evening. Nor had she married. Had there ever been a man in her life? Zanthi wondered. Had Margaret ever known physical love?

Zanthi found it impossible to imagine her secretary in the throes of passion. Perhaps Margaret had never been troubled by the needs which periodically, and to her terrible shame, racked Hyacinth. Or maybe, with typical British self-restraint and a horror of exposing unruly emotions, she had learnt to suppress, even deny, such feelings.

'Well, actually, Margaret,' she began, then without warning the door opened and Paul Benham walked in.

Hastily, Margaret straightened up, her cheeks pink, her manner shrieking guilt as she muttered, 'I'll just go and deal with these,' indicating the files. With a curt nod to the ADC, she bustled out.

Zanthi sighed inwardly. It was obvious from Paul's expression he believed they had been talking about him. What an ego, she thought, then felt suddenly uncomfortable, her stomach tensing as if under a blow. *Standing on her doorstep yesterday evening, Garran Crossley had made exactly the same comment about her.*

Shying away from the memory, and all the disturbing feelings it provoked, she glanced up at Paul.

'Well, now.' Paul smiled but there was no humour in it. 'You certainly seemed to be enjoying yourself last night.' He thrust both hands into the pockets of his lightweight trousers, their razor-sharp creases echoed in the short sleeves of his lemon polo shirt.

Even his civilian clothes looked like a uniform, and it suddenly occurred to Zanthi that Paul's self-image depended upon such details. Authority hung on him like a badly fitting suit and he seemed permanently conscious of both it and his position. He used other people as a mirror, hungry for their deference to his rank, wanting them to envy his close contact with the Governor.

Unbidden, an image of Garran Crossley sprang into her mind, a man sure of himself in any company, lowly or exalted. But the greater part of *his* life was spent roaming the wildest, least hospitable parts of the earth. He worked alone and clearly did not *need* anyone.

Zanthi felt a funny tug inside. She had learnt a hard and bitter lesson, that people were rarely what they seemed. And that to trust was to invite pain and disillusion. She was slightly startled to find herself wondering if the same thing had happened to Garran Crossley. Despite the friction between them, the wariness and reserve, there had been moments of surprising closeness, of *recognition* . . .

'That good, was it?' Paul's tone was full of pique and resentment, and it brought Zanthi out of her reverie with a jolt.

'Sorry, Paul, I was thinking. What did you say?' She met his sulky gaze calmly.

'I said,' he repeated with exaggerated patience, 'that you appeared to be having a particularly good time last night.'

'I think it was a successful evening,' said Zanthi levelly. 'Mr Crossley met everyone he was supposed to meet and the Ministers were obviously impressed by him.'

'They weren't the only ones,' Paul muttered.

Zanthi didn't reply. Anything she said would be used against her, he was in that sort of mood.

'Anyone would have thought he had you on a lead the way you trailed round after him, hanging on his every word, all smiles and secret glances.'

'I'm surprised you had time to notice.' Zanthi managed to hold her voice level and her temper down. 'I was doing my job, Paul, no more, no less.' She ignored the tiny pang of conscience reminding her that wasn't *quite* all there was to it. 'Naturally I stayed with him all evening. He had thirty people to meet and I had to provide him with background information and keep him moving.' Despite her resolve, Zanthi could feel the tension growing within her.

'OK, OK. But you needn't have rushed away like that at the end.'

'I was tired,' she replied abruptly. 'I'd had a long and exhausting day.' And you don't know the half of it, she added silently.

'I was going to take you home.' He sounded aggrieved.

'No, you weren't,' she retorted, the words out before she could stop them.

'Yes, I was,' he argued. 'I was on my way over to you when—'

'That's not what I meant.' She was about to

83

add 'and you know it,' but managed to stop herself in time. There was no point in adding fuel to the flames. 'You have never taken me home, Paul. I like to think we have a good working relationship,' she crossed her fingers, out of his sight in her lap, 'but that is as far as it goes. After all,' she added firmly as he opened his mouth, 'you already have commitments.'

Paul leaned forward, resting his palms on the edge of her desk and enveloping her in a cloud of cologne so sweet it made her catch her breath.

'You don't have to worry about that,' he said softly, his pale eyes bright and knowing, one side of his mouth twitching in a smile that was both smirk and sneer. 'It's purely business.' He winked. 'Call it insurance. In fact,' he blew his breath out in a sigh, 'it's becoming a bit of a chore.'

Zanthi recalled the hectic flush on Lady Fiona's pallid, papery, cheeks and the fevered look in her eyes, a mixture of need, fear, self-loathing and bewilderment. *Margaret had been right.*

Disgust at the mercenary callousness of Paul's behaviour rose in her throat, burning like acid. Her palm itched to slap the shiny red face in front of her. With a superhuman effort she managed to keep her feelings from showing in her expression, but her voice dripped contempt as she answered him. 'You'd

84

be wasting valuable time, Paul. I'm sure I don't qualify as a rung on your ladder to success.'

His smile broadened and she realised, hardly able to believe it, that his conceit was so great that he was oblivious to her revulsion. *He had taken her words at face value.*

'Don't sell yourself short, sweetie. With you it would be total pleasure.' He thrust his face towards her, lips puckering.

Reacting instinctively, without thought for the consequences, Zanthi flung herself backwards and leapt to her feet. Her chair kept going, collided with the wall and bounced off, the seat spinning on its supporting column.

Paul jumped, startled by her sudden movement, then his eyes narrowed and his mouth thinned to a white gash. As he drew a breath the door opened and Garran Crossley entered.

'I hope I'm not interrupting.' His deep voice, smooth as cream, held just the right degree of polite enquiry. But as he met Zanthi's wild gaze he became utterly still.

She saw his features freeze, as cold and hard as stone. In that split second he had summed up the situation and drawn his own conclusions. *But were they the right ones?* She was suddenly aware of her clenched fists, the hammer of her heartbeat, and the outrage that had set her whole body aquiver. Had he seen her reaction for what it was? Sheer horror and repugnance? Or had he put an entirely different interpretation on the highly-charged atmosphere?

The impact of his personality and physique were like a knockout punch. Last night he had been suavely handsome in his dinner jacket. This morning, in faded jeans and a fawn safari shirt whose open neck and short sleeves revealed deeply tanned skin and crisp dark hair curling at the base of his throat and on his muscular arms, he took her breath away.

Zanthi was tempted to explain, to make him hear the truth. She would hate him to think . . . why did it matter what he thought? The question echoed through her mind, resigned, relieved, despairing. In a day or so he would be on his way into the mountains and it was unlikely she would ever see him again. It was better that way. Because of their jobs their paths had crossed briefly. But the sooner he went, the better, before she made an even greater fool of herself.

Her mind flew back to their parting the previous evening and her flush deepened. She had been as jumpy as a kitten all morning, tensing every time the door opened, ears straining at each voice in the corridor, not knowing whether she dreaded or longed for him to appear. And now he had. But what was he thinking?'

The corners of his mouth tilted upwards, but the smile did not melt the ice in his eyes.

Zanthi felt her skin crawl and the hair on the back of her neck lift. Surely he could not believe she had *invited* Paul's approach? Her stomach was still churning at the ADC's disgraceful admission, and as for the thought of that wet, avid mouth on hers—she shuddered. She would as soon kiss leeches. 'No, Mr Crossley.' Nervousness made Zanthi's lips stick to her teeth and she had to moisten them. 'You are not interrupting anything.'

Garran switched his gaze to Paul, who had drawn himself up to his full height yet still had to tilt his head back to meet the newcomer's cold stare.

Chin thrust forward, hands clasped behind his back, Paul rocked on the balls of his feet. 'We have a little custom here at Government House, Crossley,' he announced, his tone patronising, his smile insincere.

Zanthi closed her eyes in resignation, momentarily shutting out the sight of her superior. She heaved an inward sigh. He was as pugnacious and strutting as a bantam cock, *and about as threatening.*

'We usually knock on closed doors, and wait until invited before entering.'

Zanthi's eyes flew open. 'Come off it, Paul.' The words were out before she could stop them, and her tone flatly contradicted his statement. All the staff had complained at one time or another about him creeping along corridors, lurking outside doors, and walking

87

into offices without even a courtesy knock.

He glared at her. 'My position is somewhat different,' he said crisply. 'It is part of my job to keep everything running smoothly, make sure people are on their toes and working hard instead of wasting time gossiping.'

Zanthi made no reply. She knew the real reason had more to do with his enjoyment of power and his insecurity.

Garran Crossley's smile reminded her of a shark as he replied quietly, 'I'll bear your suggestion in mind, Lieutenant Benham.'

Beaming with satisfaction at this easy victory, Paul clasped his hands together, rubbing the palms in a show of hearty bonhomie. 'Fine. Great. Now, tell me,' he flicked a sly glance at Zanthi before assuming an expression of concerned enquiry, 'did you have a good time last night?'

Garran's expression did not even flicker. 'It was,' his eyes met Zanthi's for a split-second, 'from start to finish, a most interesting and instructive evening.'

Swallowing, Zanthi lowered her head and stared blindly at her desk-top. *Oh, God, what did he mean by that?*

'Only—' Paul allowed perplexity to creep into his tone—'I didn't see you leave.'

'Was there any reason why you should?' Garran asked coolly.

'Well, I do try to make a point of talking to all His Excellency's guests. But somehow I missed you.'

'Don't let it worry you,' Garran's tone was satin-smooth. 'After all, we did exchange the necessary pleasantries on my arrival.'

That was one way of describing an unspoken declaration of war, Zanthi thought, suppressing a giggle of pure hysteria. It was clear that Paul hadn't actually *seen* Garran and herself leave together and was desperate to find out whether they had.

'So your evening was a success?' Paul pressed.

'Very much so,' Garran replied. 'I met everyone connected with the project, plus,' he added with a bland glance at Zanthi, 'one or two others who weren't.'

Zanthi's nails dug into her flesh.

'And what about our lovely Assistant Secretary?' Paul demanded archly.

'What about her?' Garran's tone was pleasant. But as she glanced up, Zanthi saw that his eyes were curiously opaque.

A roguish smile widened Paul's mouth and, at the bright, brittle gleam in his small eyes, Zanthi felt a stirring of dread. 'I hope she proved entirely satisfactory?'

There was no mistaking the implication. Paul was taking his revenge on her for rejecting him. But even he couldn't know how devastating his jibe was as she relived last night's parting from Garran, her gauche, impulsive offer of her mouth and his gentle but definite refusal. A scalding tide of embarrassment flooded over her.

Her eyes met Garran's for one agonising instant. She saw a flash of icy contempt and felt herself shrivel.

Then, in a movement so fast it was just a blur, Garran's hand shot out, grasped the front of Paul's immaculate shirt, and hauled him forward.

Crimson-faced, the bunched material almost strangling him, Paul gasped for air, his mouth opening and closing like a fish.

Bewildered, appalled, Zanthi could only stare at them.

'I believe you owe Miss Fitzroy an apology,' Garran remarked in the same quiet, pleasant voice. But it contained an undertone that made Zanthi's blood run cold. A brief spasm crossed his face. Was it disgust at Paul or regret over his own hasty reaction? She had no way of knowing.

Garran released his grip and Paul stumbled backwards. The whole incident had been so unexpected and so brief that just for a moment Zanthi wondered if she had imagined it.

Paul straightened his shirt then smoothed his golden hair. 'What on earth is the matter with you, Crossley?' He was visibly shaken, but managed to sound both angry and accusing. 'I was only following up what you said last night. Can't you take a joke?'

Zanthi's gaze flew to Garran. Though she

90

hated to admit it, Paul had a point. 'Miss Fitzroy suits me perfectly,' Garran had said, and she had taken him to task for it the moment they were alone.

As Garran took a step forward, Paul's hands flew up in automatic self-defence. 'You mean I've misunderstood you *again*?' Garran enquired silkily. 'I'd have sworn *the joke*,' he spat the words out, 'was aimed at Miss Fitzroy rather than at me.'

Paul began to splutter but, before he could get a word out, Garran spoke again, looking mildly puzzled. 'Surely courtesy and discretion are essential to a man in your position?'

Paul's face mirrored his confusion. 'Well, of course,' he blustered. 'I mean—'

'But you don't waste them on the staff, is that it?'

Zanthi caught her breath, and Paul flinched as the shaft slid home like a greased stiletto blade.

The buzz of the internal phone made her start, but it also broke the tension which had held her immobile as if under a hypnotic spell. She snatched up the receiver, clearing her throat twice before she was able to say, 'Assistant Secretary's office, Miss Fitzroy speaking.'

Lady Fiona's voice rasped down the line asking if Lieutenant Benham was there and if so would he go to her private sitting-room.

'I'll tell him, ma'am. Yes, right away.'

91

Replacing the receiver, Zanthi looked across at Paul, careful to keep all expression out of her face and voice. 'Her ladyship would like to see you upstairs.'

Paul nodded briefly, acknowledging the message, then turned to Garran. 'Look, Crossley,' there was an odd urgency in his tone, 'maybe I was a bit out of line. If so, I'd like to try and make amends.'

'You don't owe *me* a thing.' Garran's tone was flat.

'All right, OK.' Paul swung round to glare at Zanthi. 'No offence intended. If I said anything untoward, I apologise. Now,' he turned back to Garran, 'can we move on?'

'Gracious as ever, Paul,' Zanthi murmured, and drew her chair forward to her desk.

'Don't let me detain you,' Garran said to Paul, then turned to Zanthi. 'I need a four-wheel-drive vehicle. Can you help me with that?'

The sudden and unexpected return to normal business threw Zanthi for a moment. Then relief overwhelmed her. 'Of course,' she said simply, flicking through the circular card index. 'When do you want it, and how long for?'

'First thing in the morning if possible, and I'll need it for a month at least.'

Zanthi nodded and reached for the phone.

'So, when will you be off into the mountains?'

Though Paul's question was perfectly reasonable, Zanthi had known him long enough to realise at once that there was more behind it than polite interest. As she made her enquiries, she tried to keep one ear on the conversation taking place in front of her.

'In a day or two,' Garran replied non committally.

'Do you carry out these surveys single-handed?' Paul asked.

'Usually. Though it does depend on the type of survey required, and the terrain.'

'Surely you'll need assistance on this one?' Paul pressed. 'The interior of Jumelle is pretty rugged. You've only to look out of the window to see that. There are chunks of it that have never been properly explored. The mountains are almost entirely covered in rain forest, and there's a dangerous volcanic area where poisonous gases seep out of the ground.'

'It sounds as though you know it quite well,' Garran observed. 'Have you been into the mountains often?'

Paul sighed and shook his head. 'It's one of my great regrets. Since my arrival here I've been kept so busy there simply hasn't been an opportunity.'

Swiftly, Zanthi choked off her anger at this blatant lie. It was no business of hers what excuses Paul made for knowing so little about the island.

'It's not exactly a tourist area,' Paul went on.

93

'In fact, it's pretty damned uncomfortable from what I've heard. The Caribs don't seem to mind, though. Best place for them.' He lowered his voice. 'They have some very antisocial habits. Still, as long as they stay up there and keep out of town, I suppose we must live and let live.'

This brazen hypocrisy incensed Zanthi. Paul's fervent dislike of the Indians who had originated in South America and were the first inhabitants of the island was an open secret in Government House. She covered the mouthpiece with her hand. 'Wouldn't you be antisocial if you were confined to a reservation only a fraction of the size necessary for your traditional way of life, *and* in conditions that reduced you to the level of an animal?'

Paul turned to her. 'You've seen all this, I suppose?' he scoffed.

'Yes,' Zanthi responded tartly, 'as a matter of fact, I have. Some of the workers on my father's plantation come from the Reservation and I've taken food and medicines up there more than once.'

'How generous,' Paul's smile was venomous. 'Still, the quicker they get well the less it costs in lost production. Isn't that so?'

Flinching under the bitter cynicism, Zanthi lowered her eyes. It was her own fault. She should have kept quiet. She knew Paul envied her background, which he saw as one of wealth and privilege. It was probably one of the attractions she had for him. He knew nothing of the price she had paid, first for belonging and then for abandoning it. Nor would she ever tell him.

'In any case,' he went on, 'this does not concern you. So kindly stay out of it and get on with finding Mr Crossley a car.' He turned to Garran once more. 'Now, where were we?'

Furious with herself for allowing Paul to get under her skin, Zanthi spoke directly to Garran before Paul could add anything else. 'You have a choice of three: a small jeep, a long-wheelbase Land Rover, or a Shogun diesel turbo.'

'Well,' Paul began, 'I would—'

Without looking at him, Garran made a brief motion with one hand which, to Zanthi's amazement, silenced Paul.

And there it is, she thought, genuine authority. Never had the difference between the two men been so starkly clear.

Garran's black brows met as he thought hard. 'Make it the Shogun,' he decided. 'There will be nights when returning to town or reaching a rest-house or hotel won't be possible.'

Zanthi nodded, relayed the message, jotted a couple of notes, then replaced the receiver.

Paul's mood had undergone another lightning change. 'It all sounds like quite an adventure,' he said with an enthusiasm that surprised Zanthi. She had never known him show any interest in outdoor life, or in any kind of sport or exercise. One of his favourite sayings was that an active sex life was all the exercise a man needed.

'Oh, it is,' Garran replied drily. 'Hacking your way through virgin rain forest, soaked to the skin, with a fifty-pound pack on your back, is the easy bit. Cuts, bruises, and insect-bites are occupational hazards. Trying to light a fire with wet wood in order to get a hot drink or meal is something one grows used to, like sleeping in damp clothes and finding your boots covered in green mould in the morning. It's setting up the instruments and taking sightings on a mist-shrouded mountain that causes the odd problem.'

Zanthi pressed her lips together. It took all her willpower not to laugh at the expressions chasing each other across Paul's face.

He managed a weak grin but she could tell it had cost him a lot of effort. 'Still, it's not for long, is it? Besides, a bit of discomfort now and again makes one really appreciate life's little luxuries.'

Zanthi's eyebrows lifted. What was he up to?

'Indeed it does,' Garran agreed smoothly. 'As a matter of fact, I will need an assistant for this trip.'

Paul rubbed his hands together briskly. 'I thought you might. And as I could do with

96

putting some distance between myself and a situation which is becoming rather a bore,' he pointed with heavy significance at the phone, 'it looks as though we could do each other a favour.'

Zanthi blinked. So *that* was what he'd been angling for, escape from Government House and Lady Fiona's demands.

She sighed quietly. It would, of course, mean even more work for her, but that was a small price to pay for having Paul out of her hair for a while. Her spirits began to rise, making her suddenly aware of how oppressive the atmosphere was with him around. It would be like a holiday. She felt a moment's pity for Garran Crossley, but quickly crushed it. Sympathy was the last thing he needed. He would have Paul sorted out within five minutes of setting off. And who could tell? The experience might even do Paul good, make him a nicer person. Anything was possible. After all, hardship and challenges were supposed to be character-building.

Zanthi sobered as another thought struck her. Perhaps Paul's absence would give Lady Fiona a chance to come to her senses *before it was too late.*

Garran switched his gaze to Zanthi. 'I discussed it with His Excellency this morning,' he said, as if Paul had not spoken. Why tell me? Zanthi wondered. Why wasn't he addressing Paul? 'He had reservations at first, but those were concerned mainly with redistribution of work and responsibilities.'

'I can manage,' Zanthi said quickly. Paul wasn't going to be able to lay the blame on *her* if he got cold feet and started looking for excuses not to go. 'Between us, Margaret and I will be quite—'

'Of course, there was the problem of certain social functions,' Garran continued relentlessly, his eyes boring into hers, 'which, I now realise, can be particularly demanding.' Zanthi coloured.

'But that's what we have Honorary ADCs for,' Paul interrupted impatiently. 'To share the load and take some of the pressure off me.'

'Exactly the point I made to His Excellency.' Garran smiled, and Zanthi was aware of a faint sensation of unease, like a cold breath on the back of her neck.

'And the Governor agreed?' Paul demanded, his face relaxing into a relieved grin as Garran nodded.

'They will divide the social duties between them, leaving you free to concentrate on correspondence, administration, and all the office—'

'Just a minute,' Paul broke in, still grinning. 'You've got your lines crossed. I won't be doing all that stuff.'

Zanthi's unease grew stronger, sliding icy tentacles through her insides as she watched Garran. Her breathing grew shallower, her eyes widened.

'Oh?' he said politely, his expression still set in the same pleasant smile. 'Then what will you be doing?'

Paul laughed. 'I'll be with you, of course.'

'I don't remember saying that.'

Zanthi stopped breathing altogether. Oh, no.

As Garran's words sank in, Paul's smile faded. He swallowed. 'You did. You said—'

'I said—' Garran did not raise his voice or alter his tone—'that I needed an assistant on this trip.'

'Precisely.' Paul relaxed again.

'I did not say I would be taking you.'

Paul's face worked as he struggled to make sense of what he was hearing. 'Not me?' His voice was thin. 'Then, who?'

As Garran turned towards Zanthi, his face totally devoid of expression, she felt as though she had just stepped off the edge of a cliff.

There was murder in Paul's eyes. 'You can't be serious,' he hissed.

'Why not?' asked Garran quietly, his gaze pinning Zanthi. 'Miss Fitzroy was born here, she knows the island and its people. She is fit and strong, and she has . . . other qualities.'

'Like what?' Paul demanded thickly, and Zanthi could tell he was having difficulty containing his anger and disappointment.

For the first time in her life she sympathised with him, for she too was fighting a battle.

Fighting the sudden excitement that flared deep inside her, pouring heat into her veins, making her heart beat faster and her skin glow dusky pink. Why *had he chosen her?* Why not one of the male staff, or a cadet?

It couldn't be any physical attraction. He had made his feelings on that subject only too clear. *Unless . . .* could it be that he was simply waiting until they were *really* alone, with no witnesses, no one to interrupt or interfere?

She swallowed the sudden constriction in her throat. He wasn't like that. *How did she know?* She had only met him yesterday. He wasn't. She didn't know how she knew but she was certain. Remember Jeremy, her mind mocked.

Garran glanced across at Paul. 'She's quick, intelligent, and can think on her feet,' he replied. 'I told you last night,' he added cryptically and switched his gaze back to Zanthi, 'she suits me perfectly.'

There was something in his dark eyes that turned Zanthi's insides to jelly.

'We leave in the morning,' Garran told her quietly, his tone leaving no room for discussion or argument. 'I'll pick you up at nine.'

CHAPTER FIVE

Garran changed down a gear as they bumped and lurched over the rutted road that connected Arlington with the little fishing villages strung out like beads around the southern coast and up the eastern side of the island. The worst of the damage from the previous year's hurricane had been cleared. But with plans for the new trans-mountain highway under consideration, repairs to the coast road had been kept to a minimum.

They had already been travelling for several hours. The sun had reached its zenith and was now beginning its descent down the western sky.

Garran had allowed half an hour at noon to stretch their legs and eat a lunch of sandwiches and fruit which he had provided, much to Zanthi's chagrin.

She had peeled off her boots and socks and, leaving Garran stretched out on the hot sand, had rolled her trousers up to her knees and waded slowly to and fro, luxuriating in the warm, silky caress of the water as she chewed on her sandwich, the silence broken only by the cries of the seabirds.

He had made no comment about her going off alone, for which she was grateful. She needed the few moments' solitude to adjust to

101

this sudden disruption of her life and to put some physical distance between them. Their closeness in the car was both torture and delight. On the sand, deeply immersed in her own thoughts, she had been quite unaware of his narrowed gaze following her every move.

'The most likely route will be between the two peaks,' Garran announced, hauling on the wheel to avoid a deep rut.

'How can you know?' Zanthi asked, clutching the rigid handhold above the door. 'You haven't even started the survey yet.'

'Satellite pictures and aerial photos give us a lot of information before we set foot in a place,' he explained. 'It saves time and money. Though, by the look of things, this project is going to absorb a considerable amount of both.'

'Any special reason?' Almost against her will, her interest in his work was growing. It was impossible to separate entirely her reaction to him as a man from the job he was here to do. But her fascination with what he was saying certainly helped.

He nodded. 'A bridge over Diablo.'

'*What?*' Zanthi pictured the river. During the dry season it wound, clear and calm, through a series of lakes and pools, in a gentle fall to the marshes below Arlington and into the Caribbean. But when the rains came, this smooth ribbon of water swelled in hours to a raging torrent, thick with mud and debris.

Gushing from the narrow confines of canyons five hundred feet high, the churning water tore up saplings by their roots, gouging out the river banks and flooding low-lying areas along its course.

Bridging Diablo would be a hazardous undertaking, like trying to tame an unpredictable wild animal.

'But how—? You said you'd only be here a month,' Zanthi blurted.

'I said *at least* a month,' he reminded her gently. 'And that is merely the preliminary survey. Once the civil engineers and construction gangs move in I shall have more detailed work to do.' He turned his head and looked at her for a moment. 'I expect to be on Jumelle for well over a year.' The thin material of his blue short-sleeved shirt strained briefly across his broad shoulders as he spun the wheel to avoid a pothole in the broken tarmac.

Over a year. Zanthi looked down at her lap, clasping her hands more tightly. Her outfit mirrored his own, light cotton trousers tucked into well-worn walking boots, and a thin, short-sleeved top. She had a sudden, vivid memory of his arrival at her flat that morning. A brisk tattoo on the door and a swift appraisal of her slender figure had been followed by an approving nod.

'I knew I was right about you,' he had murmured, with a half-smile as he picked up her travelling bag.

'Oh?' She had raised one eyebrow in an attempt at irony, praying he wouldn't notice the betraying heat in her cheeks.

'You dress to suit the occasion and, even better, you travel light.'

She inclined her head in a parody of gratitude.

'Of course,' he added quietly, and she thought she detected an undertone of amusement, 'I expect that's all part of your job.'

'Of course,' she agreed lightly. *If only he knew.* How she had agonised over what to wear, what to take, and what to leave behind. Part of her, an unsuspected, treacherous, deeply feminine part, was piqued by his rejection, and wanted to force him to notice her *as a woman.* The entire contents of her wardrobe and chest-of-drawers had been dragged out, picked up and discarded, seized upon and cast aside as shame and self-mockery taunted her. What a fool she was.

He had made his position clear. Whatever his reasons for wanting her, rather than anyone else, to accompany him, they did not include personal attraction. He had left no room for doubt on that score. She should be grateful. Hadn't she learnt her lesson?

But the quiet yearning, the sudden awareness that had taken her completely by surprise, was not so easily dismissed. Not all men were like Jeremy. They couldn't be, *could they*?

What had Garran Crossley meant when he said she suited him perfectly? Zanthi had sighed involuntarily, a long, shaky, wistful sigh. There was only one answer. She did not appeal to him, and so would not be a distraction.

Squaring her shoulders, she had stared at her reflection in the mirror, willing the hope out of her eyes, tilting her chin, and mentally papering over the cracks in her shell so she could pretend they had never existed. Pride was her ally. Pride forbade her to try and impress someone who had made it abundantly obvious he was not interested.

The decision made, it was easy to return all her pretty blouses and smart trousers to the wardrobe, leaving out two old shirts and two pairs of well-washed jeans, all in lightweight cotton for coolness. She had discarded all cosmetics but her moisture cream. A towel, her toilet-bag, clean underwear, and a nightdress had been added to the bag along with spare socks and a thin waterproof jacket with a hood.

She really had believed she'd got it all sorted out, clear and final, in her mind. But now, sitting beside him as they drove along the rutted road, Zanthi realised it wasn't quite that simple.

She looked out at the scenery which seemed to have changed without her noticing from the sparkling turquoise ripples of the Caribbean to the purple and sapphire rollers of the Atlantic. Surf crashed in a snowy welter of foam on to black sand fringed by stunted green shrubs and tall coconut palms that dipped and bowed before the ever-present wind.

It had been easy enough, alone in the flat, to tell herself that all she really cared about was the welcome break from an exhausting routine. The trip would be a marvellous change from the office and it was a long time sine she had been into the mountains.

But that morning, when she had answered the door to his knock and their eyes met, her heart had leaped into her throat, then hammered erratically. She had been gripped by an overwhelming sense of premonition. Like a starshell it had burst into her consciousness, illuminating all that had happened since she saw him in the garden. Suddenly it seemed there was a pattern, a purpose in the events which had brought her to this point.

But before her brain could join the separate pieces into a whole picture, the brilliance had faded, leaving her grasping at shadows as understanding retreated out of reach.

'Zanthi?' The sound of her name on his lips startled her, jolting her out of her reverie, and she turned sharply. It was the first time he had addressed her with anything other than cool formality, even though his eyes and tone of voice had mocked the protocol. 'You've no objection to my calling you Zanthi?'

She lifted one shoulder. 'It's my name,' she replied obliquely, not at all sure how she felt about anything any more.

'Zanthi,' he repeated slowly, tasting the sound. 'It's unusual. But then,' his mouth curved in the suggestion of a smile, 'so are you.' Before she could respond, he continued. 'Tell me about your family,' he asked casually. 'Have they been here long?'

'Just over three hundred years,' she replied. 'I guess I count as a native.'

He caught her eye for an instant. 'Then I'm glad to find the natives so . . . friendly.' The timbre of his voice sent hot and cold shivers through her. 'What, brought your ancestors here in the first place? And if you say a boat . . .' he warned, allowing the sentence to hang unfinished.

A momentary recklessness seized Zanthi. 'A threat, Mr Crossley?'

His eyes narrowed, gleaming. 'A promise,' he replied softly. 'And my name is Garran.'

Zanthi remembered the way she had felt when she was learning to swim and went out of her depth for the first time. Her nerves had thrilled with a mixture of excitement and terror as she reached down with her foot and found nothing there.

She ran the tip of her tongue between her top lip and her teeth to counteract the sudden dryness and concentrated on presenting the facts. 'The island was leased to the Earl of Arlington by King Charles II, then fought over by the English and French for the next hundred years. Eventually England's title to Jumelle was confirmed by the Treaty of Versailles.'

Garran nodded pensively. 'That is most interesting.' Zanthi flushed at his dry tone. 'Obviously the island's capital was established by the Earl.' She nodded, staring ahead through the windscreen, feeling his quizzical gaze on her. 'So where does your family come in?'

'Right at the beginning,' Zanthi replied. 'The family name of the Earl of Arlington is Fitzroy.'

From the corner of her eye she saw his swift glance, then he grinned. 'A *blue-blooded* native yet!'

An inner knot of tension began to unravel, surprising her. She hadn't realised how much his reaction mattered, and the relief was tremendous. His throwaway humour was exactly right. She should have known he wasn't a man to be impressed by what was, after all, merely an accident of birth. How different from the avid gleam in Paul's eyes signalling the start of his pursuit, after Margaret, in a well-meaning blunder, had regaled him with her pedigree.

She shook her head. 'Afraid not. The title is

108

held by a different branch of the family. Though to hear my father sometimes—' She broke off, sinking her teeth into her lip, furious with herself. She hadn't intended to mention her father.

'A bit of a tyrant, is he?' Garran's gaze was on the road ahead. The question, half-joking, half-sympathetic, seemed more a comment than real curiosity.

'You could say that,' Zanthi replied guardedly, adding on impulse, 'I wish I understood him. I don't know why he wants me back on the plantation. Both my brothers work with him. They take care of the accounts and all the paperwork. I mean, what would I *do*? My two sisters-in-law are busily producing the next generation of Fitzroys, and they have more in common with each other than with me.' All her hurt and confusion over the quarrel spilled out, vivid in her voice and expression. 'What does he want from me? Am I supposed to return simply to prove his authority? He's head of the family and his word is divine law?' She shook her head abruptly and, turning away, looked out of the wide window, her vision blurred by sudden, scalding tears. Damn. What was she crying for? She hadn't cried when it happened, so why should it affect her now?

'I hear there have been some protest marches in Arlington.'

This apparent change of subject, a quirk of

109

his she was growing used to, helped restore her self-control. Blinking, then opening her eyes wide to dispel the remaining moisture, she swallowed. A slight frown puckering her forehead, she looked at him, nodding uncertainly.

'Something to do with plantation owners having too much land while the poor and unemployed don't even have a patch on which to grow their own food?'

Zanthi nodded again and heaved a weary sigh. 'That's the trouble with these agitators. They try to reduce everything to a slogan on a placard.'

'You don't think the people have a genuine grievance?'

'I didn't say that,' she replied at once. 'There is poverty and hardship among the unemployed. One of the causes is that they've left their villages to come to the city where there simply isn't any work for them. Also, it's the poorer, less well-educated people who are having the most children, so the cycle is repeating itself. There is land they could cultivate, good, productive land, and the government is prepared to help with resettlement allowances and tools to get them started. But it would mean moving back into the highlands away from the city, and few want to do that. Instead, they want the plantation owners to hand over parcels of *their* land, already cleared, fenced and irrigated.'

'Who do you think is behind the protests and demonstrations?' Garran asked.

Zanthi shrugged helplessly. 'I don't know. I don't know what the answer is either. The plantation owners create not only the island's wealth, but many of the jobs. Most of the fruit, coconuts, coffee and cotton is exported, but some of it is processed here. They have also helped enormously in promoting tourism by turning some of the old houses into hotels. Then there are the service industries which provide food, clothing and houses for the workforce. Why can't people see they are all dependent on one another, instead of bickering all the time?'

'You've clearly given this quite a bit of thought,' he observed.

'I live here. It's my home,' she replied tartly, then pushed her fingers through her hair and sighed. 'Besides, reports have to go through Government Office to the UK and one can't help but notice the discrepancy . . .' She hesitated, then added, 'Paul says it's all a storm in a teacup. He's senior to me. He's been here longer than I have. And all the secret dispatches and confidential reports go through him.'

'So he should know what he's talking about?' Garran supplied.

'Yes.' She tried to sound convinced.

'But you're still not sure.' It was a statement not a question.

'I don't know.' Zanthi moved one hand in a gesture of uncertainty. 'The trouble is he's too—' She stopped, horror dawning. *She'd done it again.* She shouldn't be talking to him like this. It was government business. Nothing at all to do with him or the survey.

'Look, obviously I don't know your father,' Garran said, 'but as a plantation owner, surely he must be concerned about these demands?'

It was as if he could look into her mind, see the danger signals and, so smoothly that she barely noticed, change course.

'The pressure of running a large estate must be considerable, certainly enough on its own for most men to handle. Perhaps this additional worry . . .' He shrugged. 'A man can only take so much.'

Zanthi recalled her father's face the evening their simmering differences had flared into open confrontation and set them in apparently unbridgeable opposition to one another.

How grey and lined and suddenly old he had looked. She realised now what she had not noticed then, a new spareness in his sturdy physique, a fining-down that bordered on frailty. The force of his personality had blinded her to the erosion of his strength and stamina by the mounting stresses in his life. She saw with a new and disturbing clarity how the plantation, her mother's chronic illness, and the inevitable crosscurrents which occurred when family and business were

112

intertwined, had drained him.

Garran's voice broke into her thoughts again. 'Is your father a man who finds it hard to express his feelings? Does he take the view that displays of emotion are a sign of weakness? I don't mean to be impertinent,' he added quickly, 'these are simply ideas you might wish to consider. If he missed you and was concerned for your wellbeing, yet had to bottle it all up, maybe *his* frustration at *your* inability to sense what he couldn't admit was the cause of the explosion. So you were both left blaming each other for not understanding. As I say,' he repeated, with an unexpected diffidence she found dangerously endearing, 'I don't know your father. I could be totally wrong.'

'As a matter of fact,' Zanthi said slowly, still adjusting to an explanation which had never occurred to her before, 'I think you may have a point.'

'Being wrong?' There was droll irony in his tone.

'You?' The corners of her mouth lifted in a flicker of a smile. She shook her head briefly. 'Perish the thought.' Lowering her lashes in mock humility, she tried to contain the heady excitement aroused by their verbal fencing. It wasn't just the thrust and parry of the words themselves after what had gone before. There were other, deeper exchanges taking place, an ebb and flow, an entirely new experience

113

which mere words could not begin to describe.

'Anyway,' he went on, throwing her a sidelong glance then concentrating on the road ahead, 'for what it's worth, I made the same mistake once.' A flatness crept into his tone. 'Only by the time I realised, it was too late.'

Zanthi looked at him quickly, every nerve vibrating like a taut wire at the significance of this remark. It was the first time he had said anything remotely personal about himself. But it triggered a silent barrage of questions. Who was he referring to? His father? Or was he talking about a different relationship?

She tried to imagine him with a woman, but her mind refused to obey. Instead, she had a sudden, vivid image of herself enfolded in those powerful arms, moulded against his hard-muscled body, her fingers threaded through his dark hair as his head bent towards hers and he murmured her name in a low voice that was more a vibration felt than an audible sound.

'Zanthi?'

Still trapped in the image, her body drugged by a warm languor that pulsed outward from a molten core deep inside her, she stared at him, her eyes wide, unseeing. She wanted . . . she needed . . .

'Zanthi! Are you all right?'

She started, her breath catching in a soft gasp.

'Don't you feel well?'

114

He was frowning. Why was he frowning? Then his question penetrated the fog clouding her brain and realisation hit her like a bucketful of icy water. Her skin flamed with painful embarrassment. 'I-I'm fine.' The words emerged as a strangled croak. She cleared her throat and tried again. 'Sorry. What did you say? I was . . .' *fantasising about you—about us.* She felt her colour deepen and swallowed hard. 'I was thinking.' She shifted on the comfortable seat, flexing her shoulders and plucking her shirt from skin suddenly hot and sticky despite the constant breeze through the open window. 'A-about my father. You could be right. I never looked at things from that angle before.'

'There, is something else you should consider,' he pointed out. 'Has it ever occurred to you how vulnerable you are?'

Shaken, she looked up at him. 'Me? Vulnerable?' she repeated blankly. Then her brain started racing. Had she given herself away? Betrayed the confusion and yearning he aroused in her? Was he trying tactfully to warn her that she could all too easily be taken advantage of by others less scrupulous than himself? 'I—I—' she began.

'Listen,' he urged, 'think about it. You are the only daughter of a wealthy man, *a plantation owner.*'

'Yes. So?' She didn't understand. What had that to do with this?

'Do I have to spell it out for you?' His tone was dry.

She swallowed. 'I—I think you'd better.' She would not jump to conclusions. If he had something to say about her attitude, her reaction to him, he must say it himself.

But his words, when they came, were totally unexpected and dropped like stones into a glassy pool, the ripples spreading ever wider. 'Kidnap, Zanthi. Ransom. And perhaps even more important than the money, a blaze of publicity for the cause.'

Zanthi felt the blood drain from her face as she stared at him, her eyes widening. 'You—you're not serious?'

He frowned. 'You think I'd joke about something like this?'

'N—No, but—I can't . . .' Her voice trailed off. He was right. The possibility that she might be at risk had never crossed her mind.

'I'm sorry.' Concern drew his brows together. 'I assumed it was something your family, not to mention the Governor, would have discussed with you.'

'Well, they didn't.' Zanthi made a brave stab at humour. 'Perhaps they decided I'm really not that important.' Or was this what was really worrying her father but he couldn't bring himself to tell her? Driven by the tumult inside her, Zanthi added rashly, 'Besides, what could possibly happen to me while I'm with you?'

The look he gave her made her toes curl.

'Remind me to show you when we stop.'

Her courage failed and, unable to brazen it out, her gaze fell, thick lashes veiling her eyes as her cheeks burned. She had asked for that. She must stop baiting him, or face the consequences. She couldn't understand her own behaviour. It was like sharing her skin with a stranger. Yet the raw excitement that fizzed in her veins when he looked at her that certain way was powerfully addictive.

But she was playing with fire, and could not pretend she didn't realise. She was a grown women, not a naïve teenager. She had one emotional disaster behind her. Was she seriously looking for another?

They drove on for a while in silence, and Zanthi was grateful. She needed time to control thoughts that kept shooting off in all directions, like sparks from a blazing log.

When Garran drew the vehicle to a stop, Zanthi's forward lurch against her seatbelt brought her back to her surroundings.

Garran got out, leaving his door open, and stood on the scrubby grass on the seaward side of the road which was now little more than a narrow, deeply rutted track of bare earth and stone. Loosening his shoulders he stretched, then, resting one hand on the roof, bent his head to peer in at her, his eyes gleaming like a cat's. 'This is as far as we go today.'

Zanthi glanced at her watch and was amazed to see it was after four.

117

'Doesn't time fly when you're enjoying yourself?' His gentle irony made her grin even as she winced.

She climbed out, pressing her hands into the small of her back to ease the stiffness in her joints. They had come a long way since leaving Arlington that morning. *In more ways than one.* They might be the only two people on the island, for the rugged coastline showed no sign that anyone had set foot here before this moment. It was an eerie thought, and had connotations that aroused both fear and excitement. Swiftly suppressing both, she walked to the back of the vehicle.

Garran had the hatchback open and leaned in to grasp her bag. Zanthi's eyes were drawn to the play of muscle beneath the thin material. He dropped the bag on the ground and reached forward again. His shirt pulled free from his trousers, revealing a strip of deeply bronzed skin that paled to white at its lower edge. There was something intensely intimate about that brief glimpse. It suggested a vulnerability—Zanthi clamped down hard on the thought, banishing it. Garran Crossley was about as vulnerable as an armour-plated tank.

'I'm afraid you'll have to manage a rucksack as well as your own bag,' he threw the words over his shoulder as he straightened up, shutting the hatchback and turning the key in the lock. 'But it's not too heavy.'

'What, no porters?' Zanthi queried with

118

deliberate sarcasm. How dared he? Why on earth had he insisted she come if he believed her too weak to do her fair share of carrying?

He glanced round sharply, then relaxed into a grin that bordered on wolfish. 'Do forgive me.' His tone took on an exaggerated humility. 'It's this sexist conditioning, the effects of a traditional upbringing,' he sighed heavily. 'I blame my parents.'

Zanthi felt herself go bright red. She thrust out her chin a little more forcefully to counteract her immediate wish to creep under the nearest rock and hide. 'I am not a rampant feminist, Mr Crossley—'

'Garran,' he reminded her.

'All right, *Garran*. But I expect to be treated as an equal. I'll pull my weight. You don't have to make allowances for me. I'm stronger than I look.'

This time his smile was genuine and his eyes sparkled with laughter. Zanthi was torn between clinging to her huff, and revelling in the glow his smile had kindled within her.

'I take your point,' he said gravely. 'Shall we go?'

With as much dignity as she could muster, she shouldered the rucksack, picked up her bag, and gazed about her, filled with a blossoming sense of expectation.

Garran pushed his arms through broad webbing straps attached to an aluminium frame supporting a bright yellow rectangular

119

case and, despite its obvious weight, hefted it on to his back with an ease that spoke of long practice. Then, lifting his own travelling bag, plus what looked like a rugby-ball of knotted string, he arched one brow. 'Ready?' Without waiting for an answer, he set off across the grassy plateau and down a narrow rocky path on to the beach.

The sun had disappeared behind the mountains, and the palms and bushes cast long, dark shadows. A tumble of rocks beneath the rising cliff showed where the limestone had been eroded by wind, rain, and the constant gnawing of the sea.

The warm breeze ruffled Zanthi's hair and she turned her face seaward, breathing in the salty tang, feeling on her skin the dampness of spray whipped from the crashing rollers and flung high in the air. She sucked in a deep, invigorating breath and quickened her step in an attempt to catch up with Garran, whose long-legged stride was widening the distance between them. Her calf-muscles protested at the sudden demands being made on them. It was like wading through treacle. But she'd bite her tongue off sooner than ask him to slow down.

At that instant he paused, and from the expression on his face as he glanced round he knew exactly what she was thinking.

By the time she had caught up and they continued walking, she was slightly out of breath. 'It's ages since I've been on this side of the island,' she panted, smiling with determined brightness and silently daring him to make some comment. 'I'm a bit out of touch with tourist development. Are there any new hotels?'

'I really couldn't tell you,' he replied. 'In any case, the place we'll be staying at is quite a bit older.'

She was almost having to run to keep pace with him and realised with a tiny shiver that to maintain such speed on the yielding sand while carrying the backpack and bag, as well as the odd-looking bundle, he had to be superbly fit and immensely strong.

'Is it far?' she puffed.

'Tired?' The dark eyes taunted.

'Not in the least,' she retorted, her breath burning and rasping in her throat. 'I just need a few minutes to get into my stride. My daily routine at Government House doesn't usually include a marathon.'

'We're nearly there,' he reassured her, and she ridiculed herself for imagining a hint of tenderness in his smile. 'It's just ahead.'

Zanthi looked at the grey-white cliff topped with dense vegetation. Her expectant smile faltered and her expression grew uncertain. 'I can't see anything.'

He sighed, shaking his head. There was something in the set of his mouth that triggered faint alarm bells.

121

'All right, describe it to me,' she demanded.

His lips had a definite upward tilt as he shrugged. 'As I said, it's quite old, and comfortably large without being impersonal. It's dry and warm, and has spectacular views. Also, guests are welcome to light a fire to ward off the evening chill. What more could anyone want?'

Despite the lightness of his tone, Zanthi didn't miss the implicit warning against complaint. She decided to change the subject. 'Perhaps you could tell me what you'll want me to do when we begin the survey. Do I take notes or something?'

He shook his head, then looked deep into her eyes. 'You,' he said deliberately, 'are my target.'

Zanthi's head flew up as shock clawed at her insides with icy talons. 'I—I beg your pardon?' she gulped.

Still his gaze held hers. 'You asked what I wanted you to do,' he reminded her gently. It didn't look as though he was smiling, yet there was something about the corners of his mouth . . .

'A survey is made by measuring and plotting distances and angles. The backpack,' he gestured over his shoulder, 'contains an instrument called a total station EDM, which stands for Electronic Distance Measurement. By timing how long it takes for an infra-red beam to bounce off a prism or reflector mounted on an alloy pole, or held at chest height against the body, the EDM works out the distance and the angle of slope.'

'I see,' Zanthi nodded slowly, her thoughts racing. 'And the reflector is another name for . . .'

'The target,' he finished, his smile urbane and innocent. But his eyes glistened, betraying inward laughter which touched Zanthi on the raw.

He was trying, quite deliberately, to keep her off-balance. *Never mind trying, he was succeeding.* It wasn't fair. He was making up the rules as he went along. Or maybe for Garran Crossley there were no rules. He lived life on his own terms, answerable to no one. And yet . . . her thoughts leapt ahead, too fast for her conscious mind to follow.

'Do you ever feel lonely?' Zanthi asked him suddenly, startled to hear not only the question, but the wistfulness in her voice.

It was obvious from his expression that she had taken him completely by surprise. But beneath the shock she saw something else, and recognised its echo within herself. An apology trembled on the tip of her tongue, bland words that would smooth the jagged edges of the deafening silence and give them both an opportunity to retreat. But the look in his eyes kept her silent.

On a surface level she had merely given him a taste of his own medicine. But it went much deeper than that, and they both knew it.

'Yes.' He bit the word off and shifted his gaze, staring out to sea. In unspoken accord they started walking again.

Her heart gave an extra beat. Something had changed. Another piece of the complex jigsaw had slotted into place. But the complete picture was still a mystery. His long-legged stride had drawn him slightly ahead of her and she quickened her pace.

Men had admitted their loneliness to her before, usually sandwiched between complaints that the boss was a swine and their wives didn't understand them. Among those who were between wives, or who had never married, the soulful cry usually presaged an invitation for her to take care of them.

Why was it, Zanthi wondered briefly, that she had never met a man who wanted to take care of *her*? Maybe she had always given the impression of being totally independent, more than capable of looking after herself. She hadn't *felt* like that, yet what choice had there been, with her mother ill and her father so busy?

But Garran Crossley was nothing at all like those men. Though she recognised the significance of his admission, she sensed that, like an iceberg, there was far more to it than appeared on the surface. For the moment that didn't matter. What counted was that he had answered her honestly. Excitement and

124

trepidation shivered through her as she stumbled up the rocky cliff behind him.

She longed for a bath, a hot drink, and some time to herself. There was, so much to think about and cool, rational thought was far from easy with Garran Crossley's broad back filling her vision.

'Here we are,' he announced, and, turning, leaned down and took her hand, hauling her up on to the wide ledge.

Imagining they were at the top of the cliff, Zanthi blew a sigh of relief and grinned, expecting to see trimmed grass, and flowers, and the familiar shape of a plantation house. Then her smile faded and her eyes grew wide.

CHAPTER SIX

Zanthi stared into the gaping mouth of the cave. It was tall enough for Garran to enter without bending his head, and about twice as wide. The smooth rock floor was dusted with a light coating of sand and a scattering of dead palm-fronds.

She swung round to face him, expecting to see his mouth curved in the teasing smile that would tell her she had fallen neatly into yet another trap. But he wasn't laughing. Save for the quizzical arch of his left brow, his face was expressionless.

Zanthi snatched her hand free. '*This* . . .?' her voice rose. 'We're sleeping in a *cave*? But—you said . . . No, don't tell me,' she added quickly as he opened his mouth. Her mind raced. 'I remember what you said: "Old, large, warm and dry".' She looked around her once more, unobtrusively drawing in a deep, steadying breath.

'Would I lie to you?' His voice was low, his tone challenging and, though he smiled, the words held several shades of meaning.

Zanthi swallowed, letting the rucksack and bag slip through her fingers to the ground. He hadn't lied. It was entirely interpretation of the facts, and she had built up an entirely different picture.

'Don't forget the spectacular views.' He flung one arm wide to encompass the panorama of coastline and ocean spread out below and to either side. His other arm rested briefly, electrifyingly on her shoulders.

'You—' She cleared her throat. 'You didn't mention . . . having to share.'

He turned her towards him, his hands firm and strong on her upper arms. Tipping his head slightly to one side, he studied her through narrowed eyelids. 'I remember quite distinctly saying that there would be occasions when reaching an hotel or rest-house wouldn't be possible.'

Zanthi moistened her lips. 'I meant . . .' She indicated the bats swooping silently in and out

126

above their heads as daylight began to fade.

'Oh.' His eyes gleamed. 'I see.' His fingers tightened for an instant before he released her. 'Just think of them as mobile pest control,' he advised, moving the yellow backpack to a niche in the wall. 'Without them the gnats would be unbearable. Look, the light is beginning to go, will you fetch some water from the stream while I—'

'What stream?' Zanthi interrupted, looking round.

'Over there.' He pointed. 'You see where the far side of the cave entrance sticks out to form a sort of barrier? The stream runs down behind that.' He crouched to unfasten the rucksack. 'There will probably be a pool—'

Suspicion reared, ugly and threatening, in Zanthi. 'Have you been here before?' she demanded sharply.

He looked up, his face expressionless. 'No.'

'Then how do you know?' Her voice faltered as he straightened, towering over her, a black silhouette against a dusky sky still streaked with pink and gold in memory of the sunset. 'These cliffs are limestone,' he said quietly, 'and limestone is porous. Rainwater filters through it. The water has to go somewhere. It gathers into streams or pools, forming caves such as this one. Over millions of years the course the water takes changes. Caves that once were flooded become dry, like this one, which means that the water—'

'Yes, all right,' Zanthi broke in. 'I'm sorry. I—where are you going?'

'Down to the beach to get some driftwood. Even tropical islands are known to turn chilly after dark.' He turned away and, within moments had disappeared, leaving only the faint sound of his boots on the rocks below.

She remained quite still for a moment. A battle raged within her. Longing to know more about him and have him notice her was one thing, suddenly discovering they were to spend the night together was something else entirely. Coming to terms with that was far from easy.

An hour later a fire burned brightly on the ledge, flames licking round the base of a metal billycan and a coffee-pot Garran had suspended from a length of green sapling supported by two sturdy tripods cut from the same tree and lashed together with nylon cord.

Mouthwatering aromas floated on the night air as Zanthi ducked under the narrow waterfall where the stream plunged over the edge of the channel it had cut in the soft rock. She gasped as the icy cascade rinsed the soap from her body.

How could water from a tropical rain forest be so *cold*? Teeth chattering, she stepped out on to the ledge and swiftly towelled herself dry, rubbing hard. Wasn't friction supposed to generate heat? So why was she wasting energy? Another clash with Garran and she'd be more than hot enough.

128

'Are you nearly finished?' His voice, though several feet away, made her jump and she tried to hurry.

'On my way,' she called back, hastily stepping into her panties then fumbling with shaking fingers at the clip of her bra. Her shirt and trousers stuck to her still-damp skin as she dragged them on, but already she was warmer. Her skin tingled and she felt revitalised.

The dip had been Garran's idea. She had been reluctant at first, refusing to acknowledge even to herself the reason for her reserve.

'Look,' he had announced, 'as I am preparing the meal, you will be washing up. But that job won't be possible until after we've eaten. In the meantime there is nothing else for you to do. Besides, I have every intention of taking your place as soon as you come out.'

The thought of clean, cool water on her hot, sticky body had been very appealing, but still she had been unsure. Feeling ridiculously shy, she dug out her toilet-bag and towel. Without raising his eyes from the vegetables he was chopping, Garran had commanded drily that she stop worrying. 'One, it's almost dark. Two, the stream and pool are screened from here by the rock wall. And three, you and I are probably the only two people within a radius of five miles.'

'That's supposed to reassure me?' Zanthi had heard the note of incipient hysteria and swallowed hard.

Garran had tutted, shaking his head. 'What an ego,' he'd murmured. 'Besides,' the undertone of dry amusement had made Zanthi's fingers curl into her palms, 'even if I could see around corners, which I can't, the sight of a naked woman is not something I'm entirely unfamiliar with, and, to be honest, right at this moment I'm more interested in a hot meal.'

Speechless with indignation, quite incapable of organising her chaotic thoughts into a suitable crushing reply, she had stalked out of the cave, grateful that the darkness hid her burning cheeks.

Holding her toilet-bag in one hand, still towelling her hair with the other, Zanthi now approached the fire. Already a pile of red-hot ash had formed in the centre. She could hear water bubbling softly in the coffee-pot. Two enamel plates, mugs and spoons were set out at one side. She looked round. Where was he? 'Garran?'

There was no answer.

'Garran?' Her voice sounded unnaturally loud. Cold tentacles of fear tightened around her as she peered into the black depths of the cave.

The tall figure emerged, firelight dancing in his dark eyes, his teeth gleaming as he grinned. 'Feeling better?'

The rush of relief, surprising in its intensity, left her weak and shaking for a moment. 'Yes,' she gulped, fighting the swirling dizzyness. 'It was very refreshing.' She forced strength into her voice.

'I've just been getting our sleeping arrangements sorted out,' he announced. The reflected flames gave his eyes a demonic glow.

'Oh?' The sudden constriction in her throat made breathing difficult. She would not say another word. She had been wrong so many times in the past forty-eight hours.

'Come on,' his arm encircled her shoulders, 'I'll show you.'

It's just a friendly gesture, Zanthi told herself, her stomach churning with hope, dread, panic and excitement. It doesn't *mean* anything. It was simply to prevent her tripping him up, or falling flat on her face.

Clutching the toilet-bag and towel to her pounding heart as if they were a life-preserver, Zanthi allowed him to lead her into the darkness. They had only taken a few steps when Garran stopped. 'Here we are.'

Zanthi couldn't see a thing. 'What? Where?'

Gently he pulled her back to the side of the cave so their bodies no longer blocked the firelight. 'There,' he gestured.

Zanthi stared at the sagging ropes for a moment, then realisation dawned. That explained the bundle of knotted string.

'Sleeping bags are too hot and too bulky,' Garran pointed out, 'besides being totally unmanageable if they get wet. And I'm not enough of a masochist to want to sleep on bare rock. So hammocks seemed the ideal solution. I'm told these are direct descendants of the ones the island Indians were using when Columbus discovered them.'

Zanthi could see that one end of each hammock was tied to the same spike of rock, while the other ends were about six feet apart. That was still awfully close.

Again Garran seemed to read her thoughts for he went on, 'Deciding where to sling them wasn't easy. Apart from the necessity for secure anchor points, they needed to be far enough inside the cave for us to remain dry if it rains. But if I'd gone in any further we'd have ended up directly underneath the bat roost. You see the difficulty.'

She sensed his laughter. 'You appear to have overcome all the problems,' she retorted, acutely conscious of his strong fingers warm on the nape of her neck.

'Not quite,' he murmured ominously and Zanthi's stomach muscles clenched. 'Have you ever used one of these?'

'Of course,' she lied, and turned back towards the fire. 'Boy, am I hungry.'

His fingers tightened, holding her fast. 'Show me,' he commanded softly.

'It's perfectly simple.' Zanthi shrugged, then tried to distract him. 'I think I smell something burning. I'd better just check the pan.'

'No, you don't.'

'Well, the food must be ready by now, and you said you wanted to freshen up before we ate.'

'There's plenty of time. We're not going anywhere.' His deep voice was infinitely patient. 'Now get into the hammock.'

'What on earth for?' Zanthi demanded, openly exasperated.

'So I can see you know what you're doing. This isn't like falling out of bed on to soft carpet. An accident on this floor could mean a broken arm or a cracked skull. You'd hardly be much use to me then. Now, put that stuff down and get into the hammock.'

Zanthi carefully laid her toilet-bag on top of her towel. She could still feel the imprint of his fingers on her neck. Reluctantly straightening up again, she wiped her palms down the sides of her trousers in a gesture that betrayed the true state of her nerves. 'Which one?'

'I don't care which one.' His voice was dangerously soft. 'It really doesn't matter. They are both the same size. One is slightly nearer the entrance, that's all. Choose whichever you like and *get in.*'

Catching her bottom lip between her teeth, Zanthi thought hard and fast, trying to remember all she knew about hammocks. You had to get in diagonally, that was it, shoulders in one corner, feet in the other. Otherwise the thing simply flipped over and tipped you out.

Lowering herself carefully, she sat in the

mesh cradle, still keeping some of her weight on her legs, even though her thigh muscles protested. Slowly swivelling sideways she swung her left foot up, reached back with her right arm to pull the mesh apart and—'Ohhh!'

Garran lunged forward to catch her before she hit the ground. But his boots slipped on the sandy floor and the combination of skid, momentum and angle sent him sprawling backwards with her spreadeagled on top of him. The jolt knocked them both breathless.

It had all happened so quickly that it was several seconds before Zanthi realised that the warm firmness against her forehead was Garran's jaw and the rhythmic thud against her left ear was his heartbeat. His left leg was bent and jammed between her thighs, and her arms, thrown up to save herself, lay on each side of his head and shoulders.

As shock receded and perception returned, Zanthi found her breath quickening as strange sensations coursed through her body, drowning out the throbbing pain in her knee where she had struck it.

With a soft, barely audible sound that was almost a groan, Garran let his head fall back against the cold rock floor. One hand held her right shoulder, the other arm lay across her lower-back. As a tremor ran through him, his arms tightened convulsively, pressing her against him, grinding her hips down on to his.

She gasped at the hot, hard strength of him,

breathed in his musky scent, and an urgent, melting weakness filled her to overflowing.

Then awareness exploded inside her: Garran had led her to believe he was not physically attracted to her. That he had lied was only too obvious, the evidence in the powerful muscular body beneath hers undeniable.

Her sudden tension must have communicated itself to him. Gripping her shoulders, he eased her away, jack-knifing into a sitting position, his head bent. Quickly, Zanthi scrambled free and stood up, dusting off her shirt and trousers with unnecessary vigour and intense concentration. Her thoughts whirled, incoherent, as she tried and failed to reconcile what had just happened with his previous attitude towards her.

In a swift, lithe movement, Garran rose to his feet, and as they faced one another, Zanthi felt her skin prickle. He started forward, checked himself, and turned away. The spell was broken, the atmosphere altered.

'You're not as experienced as you would have me believe,' he chided, and moved her gently to one side. 'Watch me. You had the right idea, but I think you'd find it easier to get your shoulders in before you lift your feet. Like this, see?'

He made it look so easy. He made *everything* look easy.

Standing up again, he beckoned her

forward. 'Now you try.'

Ten minutes later Zanthi stood up. 'How's that?'

'It looks fine. Do you think you've cracked it?'

She nodded, delighted with herself. 'It's much more comfortable than I imag—remember,' she corrected hastily.

'Just don't try turning over in the night,' came his dry reminder. 'I'm going to freshen up.'

Zanthi hugged her knees as she gazed into the flames. The wind ruffled her hair and whispered over her bare arms. She could hear the crash and hiss of surf breaking on the beach below. Already normal life, her flat, her office at Government House, the protocol, the parties, dinners and official receptions seemed light years away.

This was another world, of wind and water, of bare rock and lush, green growth, a timeless, primeval world. A world Garran Crossley understood. Though she had been born here, he knew it better. At Government House the advantage had been hers. Now the roles were reversed.

She shivered but it had little to do with the wind rippling like warm silk on her skin, cooling the sudden heat in her cheeks as she re-lived the exquisite sensation of his body beneath hers. Automatically, her mind shied away. That memory evoked other, more painful memories, and her instinct for self-protection demanded she avoid both.

But though she could discipline her mind, her body was less submissive. From the moment they met, Garran Crossley had incited feelings and reactions new to her. His touch, however fleeting or casual, fanned the flame he had ignited that moment in her flat when he covered her mouth with his fingertips to stop her talking. He had kindled a yearning which frightened her, for it meant she was no longer the self-sufficient, totally independent person she had believed herself to be.

What had those few moments when she fell from the hammock meant to him? How quickly he had regained his composure! So quickly in fact, it was as if he had dissociated himself from the incident, refusing to acknowledge it had occurred. But it had, and they both knew it.

His adjustment had been so much swifter than hers. He had not withdrawn into moody silence or sullen bad temper. He had not acted as though she were to blame and it was all her fault. If anything, despite the underlying thread of tension, he had been gentler and more patient than before.

Zanthi clasped her head in her hands. For the first time in her life she was powerless. She was here because Garran Crossley wanted her here. He had arranged, organised, placated and insisted in order that *she*, and no one else, accompany him. He couldn't have known of her existence before his arrival on Jumelle. So, requesting her as his assistant must mean that she wasn't the only one their meeting had affected.

She lifted her head, resting her folded arms on her knees, and sighed softly, smiling to herself. Despite all the uncertainty that gave her a hollow, trembly feeling in her midriff, there was nowhere in the world she would rather be, and no one she would rather be with. Each moment with Garran Crossley was a voyage of discovery, both of him and of herself. There was no turning back now.

Minutes later Garran returned from his bath, his black hair wet and tousled. Zanthi's stomach was rumbling with hunger.

'This really is delicious,' she mumbled, her mouth full of stew.

'It's the secret ingredient,' Garran replied, spooning a second helping on to her plate then scraping the remainder on to his own. He settled back beside her.

'What secret ingredient?'

'A subtle blend that adds an unexpected savour.' He scooped up another spoonful.

'Fine, but what is it?' Zanthi demanded.

'A combination of fresh air, exercise, hunger, a hint of danger, strange surroundings, and the right company.' Garran's tone matched his deadpan expression. At Zanthi's sceptical glance, he raised one eyebrow, daring her to argue, and she found herself grinning.

'You might have something there,' she agreed. 'I can't remember when I enjoyed a meal so much. In fact,' she put her empty plate down beside her, sighing as she wiped her mouth with a tissue, 'I'm sorry I've had enough. It's a shame you can't bottle it. You'd make a fortune.'

'What would you charge for something priceless to one person and without value to another?' he queried.

Zanthi thought suddenly of Paul, and tried to imagine him sitting cross-legged on the cave floor, eating off a tin plate, and bathing in a rock pool. But the picture simply would not form. Then, she realised why, with startling clarity. *Paul did not belong here.* He was out of place on Jumelle. 'I take your point,' she acknowledged.

Garran reached into his bag for a sweater. Using it as a cushion, he stretched out on his side, supporting his weight on one elbow and forearm, and looked up at Zanthi. 'You said Paul Benham had been here longer than you. But how can that be if Jumelle is your home?'

Zanthi stared at him. It was unnerving the way he seemed able to pick up her thoughts. 'He came out here with the Governor and has been on the island for the past four years. I went to boarding-school in England when I was eleven and though I came home for vacations I remained there until I finished

139

university. So although I know the island and its people better than Paul does, he has been closer to the current situation for two years longer than I have.'

Garran nodded, remaining silent. As Zanthi poured their coffee, her thoughts drifted back to her time in England. But almost at once. she mentally recoiled. England meant only one thing to her. The events of three years ago had tarnished even her early recollections.

'Who was he?' Garran asked quietly.

She couldn't disguise her shock. Even as she lowered her eyes, willing the tremor out of her hand as she put the coffee-pot down slightly harder than she intended, she knew it was too late. Denial was pointless, just as a lie would have been earlier. She had never met anyone so astute. She would not insult his intelligence, or her own, by pretending she didn't know what he was talking about. She looked sideways at him, her glance wary. 'Why do you want to know?'

He drained the mug and set it down. 'I don't, particularly.'

It was not the answer she had expected. But then, nothing about Garran Crossley was predictable. 'So—'

'But you need to get it out of your system,' he broke in. 'Whatever happened hurt you badly.' She stared at him. 'You never told anyone, did you?'

Looking away, she shook her head.

140

'Why not?' Beneath the curiosity were undertones of concern and exasperation

She shrugged, attempting unconcern, instead revealing desolation. Carefully, she put her own mug down. 'No one to tell.'

He frowned. 'Surely your mother—'

Zanthi shook her head quickly. 'She was too ill to cope with that sort of—In any case,' she turned her head to look at him, trying hard to make light of it and at the same time warn him, 'the last thing I needed was anyone else telling me what a fool I'd been.'

'It doesn't take genius to be wise *after* the event,' he said drily. But there was compassion in his eyes and it brought a lump to her throat. She swallowed hard. Confession was good for the soul, so they said.

She sucked in a deep, shaky breath and, drawing her knees up, rested her crossed arms on them. 'Looking back now, I realise I was a sitting target for someone like Jeremy. I was alone in what still felt like a foreign country. There *were* relatives, other branches of the Fitzroy family, but I'd only met one or two of them, and they, quite naturally, were very busy with their own lives. So to all intents and purposes I was alone. And in spite of *appearing* sophisticated, I was really very naïve.' She faltered and stopped.

If Garran had spoken then, prompted her, or asked a question, she would have grabbed the chance to change the subject. But, perhaps

141

realising that, he remained silent. She sensed his gaze on her face, but there was no feeling of impatience. The whole night stretched ahead of them and, as he had said earlier, they weren't going anywhere.

To her surprise, she did not have to search for the right words. Now she had taken the first step, breached the barrier which for so long had dammed it all up inside her, they flowed of their own accord.

'Jeremy joined the university when I was in my second year. He quickly became very popular with both staff and students. That was one of the things about him that really impressed me. He had this amazing ability to attract people to him. By the end of his first week he'd made a whole host of friends. Pretty soon at least half the female students were fighting over him. Being shy and a bit of an introvert, I didn't stand a chance, or so I thought, and buried myself in work.' Zanthi's mouth twisted into a self-mocking smile. 'I realise now, I was just the sort of challenge he was looking for. There was no longer any fun in chasing girls who couldn't wait to get caught. But I didn't know this at the time. *God, I was so green!*' She sighed, her expression mirroring her self-contempt. 'Suddenly this gorgeous man was interested in me. Knowing him opened up a whole new world. I could hardly believe my luck! For about a month everything was fantastic. He was charming, attentive, and very . . . patient.' She glanced at Garran, colour rising in her cheeks. But apart from a barely perceptible lift of his brows, which she interpreted as encouragement to continue when she was ready, he did not stir.

Her fingers fretted at the edges of her shirtsleeves, unconsciously pleating and re-pleating the thin material. 'I—' she cleared her throat—'I had realised very early on that for many of the girls sex was something to be enjoyed with whom and whenever they felt like it, like food or music. For some it seemed to be tied up with their ideas about independence and equality. One of two were obviously determined to sleep their way through the entire male population of the campus.' She shook her head. 'That was one of the reasons I could never understand why, with so many willing girls available, Jeremy . . .' She broke off, looking away, rubbing her upper arms. 'You see, I didn't . . . I hadn't . . .' She felt her face burn. He wouldn't notice. The firelight and surrounding darkness would hide her blushes.

She struggled to hold her voice steady. 'I wanted to love and be loved. And Jeremy had made it clear he thought it was time . . . I kept telling myself that all the things I felt had to add up to love. So why was I holding back from that final step?'

Zanthi closed her eyes for a moment and

143

rested her forehead on her arms. Still Garran did not speak. Half of her wished he would. Then she would have the perfect excuse to back off, to stuff all these painful memories back into the recesses of her mind and run away from them.

But the other half was grateful for his patience and tactful silence. The only sounds were the crackle of flames, the sighing wind, and the rhythmic pounding of the surf.

Raising her head, Zanthi straightened her spine, trying to prepare herself not only to relive the shattering horror of that evening, but also for the ordeal of telling it to someone else.

She moistened her lips. 'We'd been to a concert and then to supper at a little restaurant Jeremy knew. It wasn't one of the usual student haunts. He was always careful to avoid those, even though our relationship was known, and the subject of much speculation, most of it the "what the hell does he see in her?" kind. It hadn't exactly been an easy evening. Jeremy had been in a strange mood and I was tired. There were exams coming up and I'd been studying hard. Also, we'd been out quite a bit, so I was desperate to catch up on some sleep. But he insisted we call in at his place first.' Her eyes flickered to Garran, her mouth twisting briefly in a painful smile that bitterly mocked her own gullibility. 'He said he had a surprise for me, something he'd been saving for a special occasion.' Suddenly she'd had enough. She could go no further. 'I'm sure you can guess the rest.'

His features looked as though they had been carved from stone. 'Possibly. But it would be better if you told me.' He paused. 'For *your* sake.'

'*My* sake?' she flared. 'You're dragging all this up for *my* sake? How very noble of you, suffering such unpleasantness on my account!'

Even as the words poured out she knew it wasn't him she was angry with, but herself. She should never have let him persuade her into this. She might have known what would happen. Whatever he had begun to feel for her—and surely that wasn't all delusion, there had to be *something*, the fact that she was here was proof of that—it could not survive. Her confession would destroy it. *Good for the soul?* Only if you wanted to be a martyr! She could already see his expression changing.

His eyes were black diamond, his tone implacable. 'Unless you bring it out into the open and see the whole incident in perspective, you'll never be free of it. It will continue to haunt you, contaminating all your relationships.'

'What relationships?' Zanthi shot back, struggling for control as she teetered on the brink of laughter and tears.

Garran regarded her steadily for a moment. 'Exactly,' was his quiet reply. 'So what did happen?'

CHAPTER SEVEN

Zanthi's chin came up and she met his gaze squarely. 'Jeremy tried to get me into bed with him and I refused.'

Though Garran's expression did not alter, Zanthi had the distinct impression she had somehow surprised him. But he did not question or challenge her. He made no comment at all. She realised then that he had guessed there was more to come and intended allowing her all the time she needed to tell it in her own way. Some of the nerve-stretching tension went out of her.

'It was then, for the first time, that I saw the other side of him. I think, deep down, I must always have suspected it was there, but because I hadn't wanted to see it, my conscious mind had blocked it out. Yet it must have been that doubt which stopped me committing myself.' She took a deep breath and a shudder ran through her.

'It was horrible. From being a good-looking man, within seconds he became physically ugly.' She remembered how frustration had thinned his mouth and made his eyes small and mean, suffused with blood, and how his face had grown mottled as he ranted at her, first pleading, then threatening. 'He accused me of leading him on, of being a tease, except

146

the words he used—' She broke off, biting her lip. He had been literally spitting with rage.

'I was petrified. I didn't know what he was talking about. I hadn't knowingly done any of the things he was accusing me of. I tried to tell him, but that only made him angrier. Then I realised. He was deliberately working himself up into a fury so he'd have the excuse to do what he wanted and then claim I'd driven him to it, or that I'd been a willing partner.'

She swallowed. 'As he pointed out, I was in his room. I had gone there voluntarily, and not for the first time. Who would people believe under these circumstances?' Her hands clasped the tops of her arms tightly, as if she were holding herself together.

'I knew that if I pleaded, or let my panic show—' She bent her head, unable even after all this time to actually voice the fear that still haunted her nightmares, drenching her with icy perspiration.

'I aged ten years in the next few minutes.' Her voice was hoarse, ragged with strain as memories became reality once more. 'But he never knew. While he stormed about I sat absolutely still. As his face contorted I kept mine expressionless. Eventually, when he stopped for breath, I suggested that a charge, of rape and a public trial would surely damage his future at the university. He just laughed. He said I'd never press charges. He told me to think of the publicity *I'd* be exposed to, the questions, the physical examinations, the raking over of my past relationships, whatever *they* were, in the papers. It would be his word against mine, and there wasn't a man on any jury who would convict him.'

She paused for a moment, remembering the sudden, hot surge of her own anger, the bitter sense of injustice that crystallised into determination to fight him no matter what it cost.

'I just said, *try me.*'

Zanthi re-lived the endless moments when Jeremy had seemed to be weighing her words against his desire to possess her anyway and to hell with the consequences. Rigid with tension, not daring to breathe, she had almost fainted, clinging to consciousness only by sheer willpower and the knowledge that if she let go she would be entirely at his mercy.

'Then, without another word, he unlocked the door.' She still didn't know how she'd got back to her room. Once there, reaction had hit her hard. She had been physically sick and, trembling violently, had sobbed her heart out for two hours.

'I thought that was an end to it. Obviously, under the circumstances, we were bound to see each other at lectures and tutorials, but I simply acted as though I didn't know him. I assumed that within a day or so he'd have found someone else. He may have done, for all I know. There were plenty who were more than willing. But he was determined to have his revenge. Two weeks after it happened, despite both of us knowing I was one of his top students, he failed me on an important paper.'

Garran stiffened. Swinging into a sitting position, he crossed his legs in front of him and leaned forward. 'He was your *tutor*?' he demanded harshly, his face dark with anger.

Zanthi jumped, her head jerking up, eyes wide. She nodded. 'I'm sorry, I thought I'd—that—'

'No.' Garran raised one hand briefly. '*I'm* sorry. I shouldn't have interrupted. Go on.' Though the tone was gentle, it was none the less an order.

Oddly, Zanthi did not find it hard to obey. Fatalism had taken over. There was no going back now. She may as well finish what she had started and tell him the rest.

'At first I couldn't believe it. No one could be that spiteful. I began to think my work must have been faulty. But when I checked it, I realised it wasn't. In fact, it was one of the best papers I'd ever submitted. I didn't know what to do. Though I could have afforded to fail and not have it make too much difference in the long term, it seemed so unfair.'

She looked down for a moment, pushing her hair back off her forehead in a gesture that betrayed her growing agitation. 'It took me two days to reach the decision to confront him. It was either that, or go to the Dean, which would have meant detailed explanations and would still have ended up as Jeremy's word against mine.' She broke off, moistening her lips. 'C-could I—is there any more coffee?'

Garran picked up the pot. 'Only a drop. Shall I make some fresh?'

Zanthi shook her head. 'No, really. Just a mouthful will do.' She held out her mug and saw that her hand was shaking. Wordlessly, Garran steadied it and the warmth of his fingers seemed to give her new strength.

Draining the mug in two swallows, she grimaced at the bitter taste and set it down again, clasping her hands together in her lap. 'I stayed behind after one of his lectures. He made me wait while he flirted with a pretty blonde who was angling for extra tuition on a favour-for-favour basis. When she'd gone I showed him the paper and told him I thought the mark was too low. I suggested he's made a mistake. He said there was no mistake, that I needed taking down a peg or two and he'd decided to teach me a lesson. But if I cared to reconsider my refusal, he had a bottle of wine in his room and was free for the rest of the afternoon.'

Zanthi faltered momentarily, her gaze darting to Garran who was unnaturally still. Taking a deep breath, she pressed on, the effort visible in her face and voice. 'He said he'd be doing me a favour. After all,' she coloured visibly, 'being a virgin at my age was a

150

positive social handicap, a sign of immaturity which cast serious doubt on my ability to handle adult relationships.'

Her voice dropped. 'He was so plausible. I began to wonder if he could be right. If he hadn't started to smile, so sure he'd . . .' She lifted one hand, curling her fingers into her palm to make a fist.

She dropped the hand back into her lap. 'No one will ever know what it cost me not to slap that arrogant, smirking face. I told him I hadn't changed my mind, and walked out.'

'That was all?' The words burst from Garran like bullets from a gun. 'I'm sorry,' he apologised at once. 'It's just—Look, I understand how difficult this must be.'

'It's not, actually,' Zanthi replied, surprising herself as much as him. 'At least, not as much as I thought. You're a good listener . . . Anyway,' she hurried on, 'that wasn't all. Not quite. You see,' her gaze slid away as shame at her own behaviour battled with justification, 'I had taped the whole conversation, on a miniature recorder in my open briefcase.'

Garran blinked. His jaw tightened, but he remained silent.

Zanthi's heart sank, but she carried on, struggling to overcome the tremor in her voice. 'One phone call to Jeremy, playing back part of the tape, was enough to ensure my paper received the correct mark. He actually *laughed*. He said he admired my cunning.' Zanthi's

151

mouth curled in disgust and her eyes glistened with tears. 'He said we obviously had more in common than he thought.'

The tears spilled over, leaving cold, wet tracks down her flushed cheeks. Annoyed at her own weakness, she quickly wiped her face with the heel of one hand. 'I *hated* that. But he was right. I'd sunk to his level. Naturally, he wanted the tape back. How much was I asking for it? I pointed out that without the tape I had no protection. He could fail me again. He said he'd guarantee my work high marks for the rest of the course. I told him I wouldn't cheat, and only wanted the grades I was entitled to. He was quiet for a few moments, then he laughed. He said we'd reached stalemate, but as far as the grades went, I would never really *know*, would I?' She shrugged helplessly, tears welling once more. 'But what else could I have done?'

Seizing her shoulders, Garran wrenched her round to face him, hauling her on to her knees. 'Stop it,' he ordered. 'Stop it at once.' His voice was rough, his handling almost brutal. The dancing flames heightened the fierceness of his expression.

'What you did revealed all the qualities I've learnt to expect from you.'

Oh, God, what did that mean? In an agony of doubt Zanthi stared at him, apprehension knotting her stomach.

Suddenly the lines at the corners of his eyes

and on either side of his mouth deepened. He shook her gently. 'No one could have handled it better.' His gaze was tender and full of compassion, and his voice softened as he sought to convince her. 'Zanthi, you did nothing to be ashamed of, nothing you need feel guilty about. You fell for someone who turned out to be a bastard. That has happened to people a lot more sophisticated than you. Bait it's not the end of the world, nor is it a permanent slur on your judgement. Everybody's allowed one mistake.'

He tilted her chin with his index finger, forcing her to meet his eyes. 'You handled a very unpleasant situation with intelligence, resourcefulness, and sheer guts. The last thing anyone could call you,' he added softly, 'is a fool.'

Relief and joy had been bubbling up inside her as he spoke, now they blossomed on her face, lighting her eyes and parting her lips with a soft intake of breath. The episode had been like a poison in her system. But it had gone now. He had freed her from the fear that shackled her to the past. These and a thousand other such thoughts flashed through her mind, too fast for her to capture, let alone put into words. But her eyes said it all.

His smile faded as he studied her with growing intensity.

Zanthi felt her throat grow dry. Her heart skipped a beat.

Slowly, as if drawn by a magnetism he could not resist, Garran's head came down towards hers. As his breath fanned her cheek, his fingers slid along her jaw to cup her face. Then his mouth touched hers and the world receded.

His lips were firm and warm. Light as butterfly wings, they brushed the contours of her mouth with tiny skimming kisses, building in her a suspense, a need, that became unbearable.

She reached up to capture his head, her fingers tangling in his thick hair, still wet from the stream. Her impulsive movement seemed to free him from some self-imposed restraint.

His mouth possessed hers, searing in its hunger, unleashing in her a surge of exquisite sensation that swept her along with all the power of a breaking wave.

Breathless, trembling from head to foot, Zanthi wrenched free. She felt like someone who had unthinkingly dropped a lighted match and started a forest fire. She sat down with a thump and, drawing her knees up, buried her face in her folded arms, her chest heaving with deep, shaky breaths.

Garran dropped down beside her. 'Zanthi?' There was concern in his deep voice, and something else, a harshness that betrayed an inner battle.

She turned her head, attempting a grin. It was only a kiss. 'It's all right. Really. I'm . . .'

scared stiff '. . . OK. It's just . . .'

His back to the fire, he shifted his weight to lean on his right hip and palm, his head close to hers.

'I th—thought . . .' she stammered.

'For God's sake, Zanthi,' he rasped. '*Say* it, whatever it is.'

'*All right*,' she gasped, her skin burning, tears perilously near. 'You made it very clear, the day before yesterday, that you didn't want—you were not attracted to me.' Perspiration dewed her upper lip and temples, and trickled down between her breasts. 'If what just happened is some sort of game, or your idea of a consolation prize—' Oh, God, it was coming out all wrong. 'I don't need charity, this kind or any other,' she finished with a rush.

'*Charity?*' He bit the word off, turning his head away. She could feel the tension emanating from him. Several seconds passed. He looked at her again. 'Since meeting you,' he sounded oddly formal and his voice held a dark irony she did not understand, 'I have experienced a number of emotions. But you have my word that the urge to be charitable is not among them.'

A peculiar constriction in her chest left Zanthi feeling light-headed for a moment.

'As for not finding you attractive . . .' He shook his head slowly and a muscle jumped in his jaw, catching the firelight. The corners of

155

his mouth lifted in a wry grimace, mocking the suggestion.

With a soft sigh of relief, Zanthi began to relax.

'But,' Garran's expression hardened, becoming remote, 'I have a job to do.'

Bewilderment clouded Zanthi's eyes. Why should that make a difference? His job had brought them here. It was the reason for their meeting. He seemed to be implying that his job and any development in their relationship were, for the moment, mutually exclusive. But why? Was it for her benefit? Was he trying to protect her from gossip? If so, then insisting. on her as his assistant was hardly prudent. Or could it be that surveying was particularly demanding work, requiring intense concentration? From what she'd read it didn't *seem* so, but her research had been sketchy, to say the least, and there would be aspects she knew nothing about.

Then it clicked. Maybe it had nothing to do with any of that. Maybe, like her, he had been caught unawares by the speed and intensity of their attraction to one another and wanted to give them both a breathing-space.

Zanthi felt a great rush of warmth and gratitude towards him. Working together over the next few weeks, isolated for most of the time, mutually dependent, they had an ideal opportunity to learn about one another in circumstances that would bring out both the

156

best and the worst in them. Excitement fizzed like champagne in her veins. Like a butterfly emerging from a chrysalis, she was looking at life through new eyes, fresh and eager.

She smiled up at him. 'I understand,' she said softly.

He looked at her for a moment, then his mouth compressed. 'No.' His voice was grim. 'You don't.' Abruptly, he turned away and stood up. 'Come on, let's turn in. We have a long day ahead of us tomorrow.'

Zanthi lay in her hammock, listening to the ocean and the slow rhythmic breathing of the man beside her. High in the roof of the cave the bats squeaked and rustled. She turned her head and gazed at the flickering flames, glad of their faint warmth. Sleep was a long time coming.

Over the next few days Zanthi slipped into a pattern of living with an ease which, on the rare occasions she actually stopped to think about it, amazed her.

The first casualties were the sense of urgency and pressure which had characterised her daily schedule at Government House. Their disappearance left her initially bereft and uneasy. But once she had accepted the fact that, for the first time in many long months decisions were not hers to make and responsibilities not hers to shoulder, the relief was wonderful.

No matter how early she woke, Garran was

already up and about, clad only in trousers and boots, his hair still wet from a dip in the crashing surf. Crouched in front of the fire cooking freshly caught fish while coffee bubbled in the pot, he was the first thing she saw.

Zanthi treasured the moments she was able to watch him without his knowledge. They were all too brief. For even though she did not stir, except to open her eyes, he sensed within seconds, without even looking in her direction, that she was awake. He would tell her to get moving, that it was practically lunchtime, and half the working day had already gone. She would answer in kind, bemoaning a fate which had forced her into the company of a slave-driving insomniac.

But, for those few precious moments, she could gaze on him to her heart's content and wonder at his frowning preoccupation, a concentration far greater than necessary for the routine task he was engaged in.

There wasn't an ounce of spare flesh on his powerful body. His bronzed skin gleamed with good health, gilded by the early morning sun. The urge to touch, to feel the play of muscle and sinew beneath her palms, to slide her fingers through the black curly hair that matted his chest and arrowed down across his flat stomach was a sweet, gut-wrenching torture.

There was no vanity, no trace of the poseur

in his semi-nakedness. He shaved by touch alone and his hair received a few careless sweeps with a comb only after his swim in the morning and his dip in the stream at night. If he possessed a mirror, Zanthi had yet to see it. She sympathised with his reluctance to put on a shirt until they actually set off into the forest. Then insects and the razor-sharp edges of cycads, ferns and young palms would make it a necessity.

The pull of mutual attraction that vibrated just beneath the surface of their banter, plus her own sense of modesty, forbade her to follow his example. At breakfast and supper, when the cooling wind on bare skin was bliss, all she could do was roll her sleeves as high as they would go, and leave her blouse outside her waistband to allow the air to circulate.

She knew he was aware of her discomfort. He did not miss a thing. But his lack of comment or suggestion indicated his appreciation of her tact in remaining fully clothed. Her one concession to comfort was quietly to abandon her bra, for she was unable to bear the chafing and constriction where it clung to her sweat-dampened skin. As she pushed the scrap of lace and elastic to the bottom of her bag, Zanthi smiled to herself, wondering what Margaret would have said.

Garran cooked, she washed up. He gathered wood, she rinsed their clothes in the pool each evening and hung them to dry on a

159

line he rigged up across the mouth of the cave.

They worked twelve-hour days, leaving the cave soon after sunrise and returning just before dusk. They tramped up mountains and down valleys. She carried the reflector and the rucksack with their lunch and waterproofs. He carried water-bottles and the backpack containing the survey equipment.

Zanthi quickly decided she preferred it when they worked in a triangle. At least then she had the satisfaction of seeing him scramble to take her place while he sent her to the next point. When they worked in a circle, he would set up the instrument on some high piece of ground and stay put, simply turning the instrument to face her as she stumbled through the undergrowth and fought her way around him. He would take readings every few metres and tap the figures into what looked like a flat calculator but which he said was a solid-state memory, joined to the instrument by a short, thick lead.

'There's something wrong here,' Zanthi panted at the end of the second morning as she followed him up the steep incline, her shirt sticking to her. '*I'm* the one doing all the work.'

He grinned at her over his shoulder. 'Naturally. What else are assistants for?'

'I foolishly imagined they were to assist,' Zanthi retorted. 'Why can't I stand in one place and punch the buttons for a change?'

160

'There is rather more to it than that,' Garran replied, his eyes reflecting his amusement. 'To become a surveyor takes years of training.'

'Are you awarded bonus points for the number of assistants you kill off?' she demanded.

Garran sighed, shaking his head. 'That's the trouble with today's youth, no stamina.'

'Listen, Garran,' snorted Zanthi, 'give me a week and I'll be running rings around you.'

Garran spread his hands with all the smug satisfaction of someone whose point had just been proved. 'What more could I ask? Come on, I'm sure we can manage one more set of readings before lunch.'

He started off down the mountain, leaving Zanthi gazing after him, unable to decide whether to stamp her foot, stick her tongue out, or scream with sheer frustration. She shook her clenched fist at his broad back, then, with a shrug, followed.

'That's the spirit,' he called airily without looking round.

Zanthi bit her lip. She would not laugh.

It started with a sigh in the canopy of leaves and branches a hundred feet above their heads. A sigh which became a rushing roar as the gusting wind drowned the chatter of the parrots whose green, blue and orange plumage, mimicking sun, sky and leaves, made them almost invisible.

161

Zanthi tipped her head back to look up, as the rays of sunshine that filtered through, to cast pools of golden light on the forest floor, were cut off as abruptly as if a switch had been thrown. The cool, green gloom pierced by sunbeams existed no longer. The forest was suddenly grey-dark and threatening.

'Here it comes,' she shouted to Garran, and swung the rucksack down to haul out the waterproofs. She knew without looking that he was swiftly dismantling the equipment and stowing it in the yellow backpack, which carried a warning sticker that read 'Electronics and water do not mix. Please protect accordingly.'

Zanthi pulled a wry face. That was easier said than done when working in the rain forest. There had been a downpour on each of the four days they had been here, and it wasn't even the wet season. Four days. She found it hard to believe. The time had gone so quickly. And yet there were moments when it was difficult to remember what normal life was like.

The forest grew darker. Rain hit the canopy with a thunderous drum-roll and began to cascade through the leaves. Within moments the slope beneath their feet had grown soft and muddy as little rivulets of water coursed through the leaf-mould and debris on the forest floor.

Zanthi slithered and scrambled after

162

Garran as he made for the shelter of a small, shallow cave formed by a rocky outcrop. Once under cover, they helped each other out of the waterproofs, whose positive worth was diminished by the Turkish bath effect of heat, humidity and effort, and used them to shield the backpack. It was a full fifteen minutes before the downpour began to reduce in quantity.

The drumming stopped and all around them the darkness was lifting. The scent of vegetation and wet earth was strong, and water, dripping from the glossy, freshly washed leaves, hit the ground with a steady patter. A bright beam of golden light angled down through a gap in the canopy and once more the forest echoed with flute-like trills, metallic whistles and harsh squawks as the birds resumed their territorial squabbles and courtship displays.

'Where are we going?' Zanthi asked as they skidded and slithered down the steep slope.

'Back to the cave to pack up.'

'Oh.' Zanthi received the news with mixed feelings. She wouldn't be altogether sorry to leave the forest. There had been several occasions during the past couple of days when she had been sure someone was watching her. It wasn't Garran, of that she was certain. This was different, unnerving, making the fine hairs on the back of her neck lift and her skin prickle.

163

Her heart racing, as a rush of adrenalin prepared her to fight or flee, she strained to pierce the shadows, searching for the source of her unease. But not once did she glimpse anything out of the ordinary. She thought of mentioning it to Garran, then dismissed the idea. If there was anything out there, he would have known long before she did, and he would have told *her*.

She was just a bit edgy, that was all. Heaven knew, she'd had plenty on her plate this past week. With so much to think about, the iridescent flash of a hummingbird, or a lizard skittering away beneath a fern frond, were more than enough to send her imagination into overdrive.

But, while half of her was tempted to return to the security of ordinary life, the other half didn't want this time alone with him to end. How empty her life had been before he came, always busy, yet unfulfilled. With one gentle, fleeting touch he had cracked open her shell and awakened the woman within. She had confided in him things never before shared. He had reassured and comforted as no one in her life had ever done. He had helped restore her confidence and self-esteem, and had shown her that life existed beyond the confines of her job and flat.

Already she was beginning to rely on him, not just for his practical ability and strength, but for his insight and humour, knowing that all she had seen so far was but the tip of the iceberg.

'Then,' Garran said over his shoulder, 'we go north.'

'Oh,' Zanthi said again, now even more uncertain of her feelings. They weren't going home. Clearly the expedition wasn't over yet. *But*—'That's Carib country,' she pointed out.

'So I've heard.' He sounded uninterested. 'What concerns me is the fact that it's where the geothermal area is and where Diablo's main tributary rises. Detailed information regarding both is vital to the engineers working on the highway project.'

Zanthi followed him in silence for a while, her thoughts clamouring.

'Garran,' she said eventually, 'why didn't we *begin* with the geothermal area?'

He shrugged. Directly behind him, Zanthi could not see his face. 'The new road will link the east coast with the west. One of the ministers was telling me that ideas are being discussed for a tourist complex of hotels, shops, and so on, at the fishing village of St George on the north-east coast, so this side of the mountain had to be surveyed anyway.'

'Yes, but if we'd done it the other way round, we could have followed the track out of Arlington that runs most of the way to . . .' Her voice faltered as realisation welled up like clear spring water. 'We needn't have stayed in the cave at all.'

165

Garran stiffened and swung round, a movement so sudden it made her jump. Her foot slipped and she would have fallen if he hadn't grabbed her arm, his fingers like steel clamp as he hauled her upright:

'Tell me,' he demanded, dangerously quiet, 'in the cave, were you wet and cold?'

Taken aback, she stared at him. 'No . . .'

'Did you lack food or sleep?'

'No—'

'Do you think that, if you had come into the forest for a few hours each day and returned to your flat each night, you would be as fit, or as capable of dealing with adverse conditions as you are now?'

'No,' Zanthi admitted, her voice dropping. 'But . . .'

'But what?' Garran's expression softened. His hand slid down her arm and captured her fingers, linking them with his. 'Zanthi . . .' he was uncharacteristically hesitant '. . . I had more than one reason for choosing you as my assistant.' There was a conflict in his eyes she did not understand. He paused, then, on the brink of saying something, smiled.

It was a genuine smile full of warmth. But a fleeting chill, like an icy breath, feathered down Zanthi's spine. Whatever he said next, the words would not be those he had originally intended.

'One thing you must have learnt in the last few days is that a job like this demands

166

teamwork. On our way to the cave the day we got here you told me you didn't need or want any allowances made. You could pull your own weight. Brave words, and,' he added before she could interrupt, 'you have more than lived up to them. But words cost nothing. I had to be sure. From here on, things will get tougher.'

Zanthi could not rid herself of the conviction that, despite his second thoughts, he was still trying to tell her . . . *what*?

She lifted her chin, meeting his eyes. It all came down to one simple question in the end. She forced herself to sound flippant. It was her only defence. 'Are you thinking of trading me for a . . . different model?' Someone, she thought, more used to your way of life, more competent, more experienced, more . . . everything.

His fingers tightened on hers. His voice was soft and deep. 'Not a chance.' He paused, a nerve flickering beneath his left eye. 'Do you want to leave?' Though he spoke without discernible expression, she sensed the question had depths she could not even begin to plumb.

Leave him? Just when she was beginning to . . . Her eyes widened and her breath caught in a tiny gasp. His own eyes mirrored the change and an electric current seemed to arc between them.

Zanthi's lashes veiled her eyes and she felt hot colour burn her face. His grip was almost painful. 'Not a chance,' she replied, her voice husky.

Raising her hand, he kissed her open palm. Their eyes met and Zanthi trembled. Then, releasing her, they continued their descent.

CHAPTER EIGHT

'There's only one thing.' Zanthi glanced across at him as they swayed and jolted along the rough track. 'We're hardly likely to find another suitable cave, especially in the depths of the forest.'

'I imagine not,' he agreed blandly.

'And I don't see anything resembling a tent among all the gear.'

'True.'

She twisted her hands together in her lap. 'Did your informant happen to mention a rest-house or hotel in the area we'll be surveying?'

Without taking his eyes from the track, Garran shook his head. 'Not that I recall. In fact, he made the point that few people will go near the volcanic area. Apparently, they believe the gases are evil spirits which will kill them if they are breathed in. There's no doubt that sulphur fumes are pretty potent, a powerful mixture of boiled cabbage and rotten eggs, but—'

'Garran,' Zanthi interrupted, 'where will we be sleeping? I'm not going to be difficult. I'd just like to know.'

He jerked a thumb over his shoulder. 'In the back,' he replied calmly. 'The seats fold flat. There'll be plenty of room.'

She darted a glance at him, noting the tension in his jaw and the slight compression of his lips. He wasn't quite as nonchalant at the prospect as he would have her believe. She was briefly, fiercely glad. She also noticed he hadn't offered to sleep outside by the campfire. In a strange way, she was glad about that too, for it saved her the embarrassment of confessing, with the ever-present risk of misinterpretation, that she didn't want to be alone.

The feeling of being observed persisted. She knew it was ridiculous. They were no longer on foot and they had come a considerable distance. But it wouldn't go away. Out there something was watching them. Couldn't he sense it? Involuntarily, she looked across at him.

'Something wrong?' he enquired.

She scanned his face. His features registered mild concern, *nothing else.* She had to get her imagination under control. She could have understood it better if these silly flights of fancy had occurred in the first day or two when everything was so new and strange.

She had believed she'd adjusted to the completely different life-style rather well. Obviously she hadn't. Perhaps she had underestimated the effects of all the added stress.

'N-no.' She managed a quick, bright smile. 'Everything's fine.'

He nodded, apparently satisfied.

The track curved, but, instead of following it round, Garran braked. Then, pulling hard on the steering wheel, he guided them down into a slight hollow with a stream running through it. Some time in the past trees had been felled and the area cleared, but now the forest was beginning to encroach again.

Open to sun and rain, the ground was covered in a thick carpet of coarse grass that seemed to grow flat instead of upright. As they both got out, Zanthi glimpsed, among the tall ferns at the edge of the clearing, the bright red flowers of a lobster-claw heliconia, and caught the fragrance of a ginger shrub's white blossom.

She walked down to the stream, stretching her arms high and wide, loosening the tightness in her neck and shoulders. Her nostrils twitched. The water had a funny smell, faint but unmistakable. She bent to dabble her fingers and started in surprise. 'Hey,' she shouted over her shoulder at Garran who was standing quite still, looking around him. He looked up sharply. 'This water's warm!'

He visibly relaxed. Pushing his hands into his pockets, he strolled towards her. 'Volcanoes tend to have that effect,' he said drily.

She pulled a face at him. 'It smells a bit, though.'

'That's the sulphur. It's supposed to have marvellous health-restoring properties. People pay a fortune at spas to drink and bathe in sulphur water.'

Zanthi grimaced. 'There's no accounting for taste. Still, "when in Rome" as they say.' She started to unlace her boots, noticing that a velvet dusk was banishing the last of the daylight.

Garran went straight to the Shogun, unlocked it, and switched on the headlights. 'Now at least we can see what we're doing. The first thing is to get a fire going.'

'How?' Zanthi looked round helplessly. 'We certainly won't find any dry wood here.'

'We don't need it,' he replied. Reaching into a storage compartment under the dashboard, he drew out a large, bulky penknife.

Zanthi watched, her curiosity growing, as he cut several branches from nearby shrubs and saplings. Quickly stripping off the foliage, he cut the wood into short lengths and made a pile of it. Then he crossed to a smooth-trunked tree, whose crown of leaves was a darker shadow high above their heads, and made six slashing cuts in the bark.

When he walked away and started picking up handfuls of the stripped foliage, Zanthi could no longer contain herself. 'What *are* you doing? And why did you cut that tree?'

171

'It's a gum,' Garran replied, carefully wiping the foliage across the slashed trunk. 'They ooze a flammable resin. It's an instant fire-lighter when there's no dry kindling. By the time the gum has burned away, enough moisture will have been driven from the wood to allow that to burn as well.' He pushed the resin-smeared leaves into the pile of wood and went to get some more.

'Look, there's nothing for you to do at the moment. Why don't you go and have a soak in the stream?'

'You're sure I can't—?'

'Positive,' he replied firmly, not allowing her to finish.

It wasn't until Zanthi was sitting in the water, the flow massaging her back and swirling round her waist, that she realised her dry clothes were still in her bag in the vehicle.

Her head dropped forward for a moment and her shoulders sagged as she heaved a sigh. That was what came of not concentrating. Her gaze and her thoughts had been on Garran as he crouched over the crackling fire, the flames lighting his face with an orange glow, accentuating the planes and angles and giving him a brooding, introspective look.

She shrugged, and rinsed her socks, watching the lather dissolve, swept away by the swift-flowing water. Wringing them out thoroughly, she tossed them on to the jeans and panties already folded neatly on the grass

172

and reached for the shirt anchored between her knees.

Garran had been right about the special qualities of the water. It had soothed the ache from her muscles and mellowed her exhaustion to a pleasant tiredness. She would certainly sleep well tonight.

Tonight. Her nerve-ends jangled. Tonight she would lie beside Garran. Not in separate hammocks, but in a space smaller than the average double bed. She would *not* think about it. Time enough for that when the moment came. Feverishly, she scrubbed the shirt, working up a froth of suds. Afraid or hopeful? *She didn't know.* Stop it. Think of something else.

She had washed herself from top to toe, including her hair. The combination of soap, shampoo and sulphur had been unusual, to put it mildly, but at least she was clean. A light dusting of honeysuckle talc would, she hoped, remove any persistent trace of rotten-egg smell.

In any case, Garran would hardly be in a position to complain. He's have to bathe in it too, and it was his decision that they spend the night together in the Shogun.

Zanthi's throat tightened as excitement and apprehension surged through her.

'Zanthi?'

Her head flew up, eyes widening, and, in an unconscious gesture of self-protection, she

173

clutched the wet shirt to her breasts. She swallowed hard. 'Yes?'

'Are you nearly through?' She was just to one side of the headlights' beam and could see him clearly. He had his back to her, his hands in his pockets, and his head half-turned so his voice would reach her. 'I'd like to get cleaned up before I eat.'

'Just coming,' she called back quickly. Wringing out the shirt, she tossed it on to the other wet clothes and climbed out on to the grass. Wrapping one towel around her, sarong-style, she used the other smaller one to dry her feet, then stuck them into her boots.

Garran had impressed upon her the importance of looking after her feet. It would be all too easy, given the climate and conditions, for fungal infections to develop or blisters to turn septic. Zanthi had taken his warning to heart, especially the part about never going barefoot in the forest where a snake-bite or a puncture-wound from a thorn was potentially fatal. Cleaning her boots had been her priority.

Hanging the small towel around her neck, she picked up her toilet-bag and wet clothes and clumped back to the vehicle.

Garran was bent over the fire, stirring the contents of the saucepan. The savoury smell made Zanthi's mouth water and, to her intense embarrassment, her stomach gave a loud rumble.

Garran looked up. A grin widened his mouth and he straightened, still holding the spoon. His gaze raked her from dripping head to her unlaced boots, lingering momentarily on the curve of breast and hip beneath the tightly wrapped towel. 'It might lack the sophistication of haute couture,' he observed, 'but I've got to admit that it has appeal.'

'Thanks,' Zanthi responded drily, her entire body flushed and tingling under his lazy scrutiny. She stalked past him to the open hatchback with as much dignity as her bizarre outfit permitted. Dumping her washing and toilet-bag on her waterproof, she snatched her clean clothes from her bag and, with quick, jerky movements, scrambled into them, glowering at Garran's broad back as he walked down to the stream, shrugging off his shirt as he went.

His remark was a forcible reminder that in the entire time they had known one another, which, a small voice reminded her, was not very long in terms of days, he had never seen her looking her best. At work, protocol ruled her choice of clothes, even for social functions. And here—she looked down at the creased and worn trousers, and the blouse that had clearly seen better days, and sighed in resignation.

Perhaps there were advantages. With his having seen her looking her worst, any change could only be an improvement.

175

Garran returned from his bathe, and they ate their meal sitting side by side on a ground sheet. Between mouthfuls of tinned stew and bananas, washed down with coconut milk, they talked.

'There are no pure-bred Caribs left on Jumelle now,' Zanthi said, in answer to one of his many questions. 'The people who live on the Reservation have intermarried with Africans who were imported here as slaves, and with Europeans. Even their language has died out.'

'Were they a peaceful people?'

Zanthi threw him a wry smile. 'Hardly. The word "Carib" is also the basis of "cannibal".' She paused. 'With some tribes there is a great deal of respect and ritual attached to eating their enemies. The belief that you take in all their good qualities, courage, marksmanship, tracking ability and so on, is just one example.'

'And the Caribs didn't take that view?'

Zanthi shook her head. 'They just liked the taste of human flesh.' Her mouth twisted in distaste. 'One of their customs was to preserve the arms and legs of their victims for eating at a later date by smoking them over wood fires. They even ate the babies they fathered with Arawak women, whom they took as slaves after killing their men.'

Garran's eyes rolled up and he slowly keeled over sideways, hitting the ground with a thud.

Zanthi stared at his crumpled body, uncomprehending. Throwing her plate and mug aside, she knelt and turned him over on to his back. 'Garran?' She patted his face tentatively. A lock of black hair had fallen across his forehead and his jaw was rough with beard-stubble. 'Garran?' Her voice rose slightly. She shuffled forward, heaving him up until his shoulders were resting on her legs. 'Say something,' she entreated under her breath. Cradling his head against her breasts gave her a peculiar feeling, a wonderful, powerful feeling.

He opened one eye. 'Gotcha.'

She gasped, shock mingling with relief. Then, as he grinned, realisation dawned and she snatched her hands away, letting his head fall. He rolled off her lap, shaking with laughter. 'You rotten, horrible—' she exclaimed, giving him a forceful push. 'Of all the lousy tricks . . .'

He lifted his head, craning his neck to look round at her, his dark eyes gleaming in the firelight. 'I know,' he spluttered, 'but I just couldn't resist it.'

Zanthi tried to stop herself laughing back, failed, and thumped him again.

He contorted his face in mock agony, raising his arms to protect himself. 'This is no way to treat a superior.' He was still laughing.

'*Superior?*' she cried indignantly. 'I'll give you—'

But, before she could complete her threat, with one sinuous, twisting movement he had rolled over and pinned her to the ground, her arms immobilised above her head, his face barely a hand's breadth from hers.

'You'll give me . . . what?' he demanded softly.

It wasn't only her body that was trapped. His dark gaze mesmerised her, sapping her will to move. In the depths of his eyes something stirred. Tension rippled through his body and Zanthi felt herself respond. She was melting in his heat, becoming soft and pliable, her body moulding to fit the contours of his. She wanted to be closer . . . closer.

He shuddered and bent his head, his eyes closing as he rested his forehead on her shoulder. A barely audible sound forced itself from deep in his throat. Distantly, she sensed the battle raging in him, but could not help. She was being drawn down inside herself, into unexpected realms of delicious sensation that curled like smoke and sent tiny shivers along every nerve. She was burning, drowning, falling, and she wanted . . . oh, how she *wanted*.

'Garran, please—' The sound of her own voice, half-pleading, half-fearful, was a shock to her. She opened her eyes and met his piercing gaze. She could only stare back, mute, helpless.

Time seemed to stand still, then his lips brushed her cheekbone, a touch as light as thistledown.

'Zanthi . . . I'm sorry,' he rasped. Rolling away, he sat up, his back to her, head bowed. 'I didn't intend—'

'*Don't*,' she interrupted. After a fractional hesitation, she laid her hand on his shoulder. 'The last thing I want is an *apology*.'

Turning his head, he looked hard at her, searching her face. She rested her chin on the fingers spread against his shirt. 'Oh, Garran—' Her voice was a hoarse whisper as she struggled to find words which would convey the immensity of what was happening to her.

'I know,' he said quietly. It was not offered as comfort or reassurance, though it conveyed both. It was a simple statement of fact. But, even more than that, it was an acknowledgement of his own feelings.

Her heart gave a painful lurch that stopped her breath for a moment. 'But?' she murmured.

He gave one brief shake of his head. 'Not here, not now.' He seemed to be trying to convince himself as much as her.

Why not? Zanthi caught the inside of her lip between her teeth. But the question hung in the air as clearly as if she had spoken.

'The consequences—' He shook his head again, driving one hand through his hair, revealing a frustration that shook her, such was its bitter intensity.

Zanthi flushed scarlet. Utterly absorbed in

the glorious feelings he had ignited, and urged on by forces beyond her control, the thought of risks or consequences had not once crossed her mind.

'Oh, Garran, I'm sorry,' she whispered, stricken with remorse.

He looked over his shoulder at her. '*You're* sorry?' The irony in his tone was reinforced by a twisted grin.

'I should have realised—'

'For God's sake, don't you start apologising!' he grated.

'But the responsibility was—is—half mine,' insisted Zanthi.

His left, brow lifted. 'OK, so it's half yours,' he agreed. 'Does that make you feel better?'

'No.' At her helpless little shrug he started to laugh and she sensed an easing of strain.

'Oh, Zanthi, what am I going to do with you? No, don't answer that.' He raised one hand in a fending-off gesture. 'My self-control has its limits.'

'Spoilsport,' she murmured, peeping up at him, an impish grin hovering at the corners of her mouth. Garran Crossley, I'm falling in love with you: as the knowledge flashed into her mind she felt her expression change. Her eyes widened and her smile faded. It was too soon. *What had time to do with it?* She knew so little about him. That wasn't true. She might not know details of his past but, whatever his background and experience, they had made him the man he was now, the man who captivated her totally.

He held her gaze for a moment, his jaw tightening. 'Wash the dishes, woman,' he growled. Rising swiftly to his feet, he strode round to the back of the Shogun and began hauling all the gear out on to the ground.

Zanthi knelt at the stream, scouring the pan with fine gravel scooped from the stream bed. She was about to rinse it when something, she wasn't sure what, put all her senses on full alert. She listened intently, her eyes wide as she scanned the shadows for the slightest suggestion of movement. She could hear and see nothing at all suspicious. It made no difference. She knew someone was watching her. She was certain of it.

She looked over her shoulder, automatically seeking Garran. His profile towards her, he was standing near the fire, turning the washing on the makeshift line to dry the other side. By the time the rain came in the morning their clothes would be dry. He appeared totally engrossed in the task, and once again Zanthi wondered. *Could* it be just her imagination? The surfacing of repressed childhood fears? Even as the thought occurred, the prickling awareness faded and disappeared. Zanthi turned back to the pan.

'Here.' Garran touched her shoulder lightly and handed her a mug of fresh water from their drinking supply. 'For brushing your teeth.'

181

She smiled up at him. 'I was just wondering about that.'

While she cleaned her teeth he took the dishes back, then passed her, carrying his own mug and toothbrush. As Zanthi returned to the Shogun, despite all her resolve to treat the arrangements as a logical response to circumstances, her heart was beating faster and her throat was so dry she had to keep swallowing.

The two sets of back seats were folded down and Garran had stowed all their gear at the front to leave them enough room to stretch out.

Zanthi tugged off her boots, found a narrow space for them at one side, and crawled in through the open hatchback. She lay down on the thick, padded upholstery and heaved a deep sigh that combined relief and gratitude. Hammocks had their good points, but for real comfort you couldn't beat lying flat. Closing her eyes, Zanthi indulged herself in a long, luxurious stretch.

'Comfortable?'

Her eyes flew open. Garran was gazing down at her. The dry amusement in his smile echoed that in his voice, but his eyes were unreadable.

'Y-yes, thank you.'

'Well, move over. I'm all for equality, but with my height and build I need a little more room than that.' Without waiting for her reply he slammed the hatchback shut and opened the offside rear door. Removing his boots, he stowed them in the front, on top of the backpack, switched off the headlights, and climbed in beside her.

In the glow from the firelight Zanthi watched as he eased himself down. Flat on his back, his knees bent, he groaned with relief. 'God, that's better.'

They lay side by side in silence for a while, but gradually Zanthi became aware of a discomfort she had been trying to ignore. It was no good. She would have to go.

Sitting up, she began to pull on her boots.

Garran propped himself up on his elbows. 'Where—?' he began, but at Zanthi's pointed look, grinned. 'Sorry. Will you be all right?'

'I think I can manage by myself,' she retorted with light irony, glad the firelight hid her crimson cheeks. This was embarrassing enough, without the implication that she needed him to hold her hand.

But, as she clambered out into the darkness, she shivered. There was something about this place. She hurried to the bushes at the edge of the clearing, keeping the vehicle between herself and the fire in the hope of added privacy.

The forest canopy whispered and sighed high above her head and she could hear the scuffling of tiny nocturnal animals. Around the clearing the darkness and tall trees formed an impenetrable wall and Zanthi's heart was thudding like a steam-hammer as she ran back to the Shogun.

The interior light was on and the door opposite hers was open. Of Garran there was no sign.

Zanthi climbed in. Obviously, he'd decided to follow her example. She sat down and lifted one foot to tug off her boot. A noise from outside made her look round. Her eyes widened and a scream rose in her throat.

CHAPTER NINE

'Hey, boss, look what I foun'!' The sing-song Creole accent came from her other side. She whirled round. A brown face, sheened with greasy sweat, leered in at her. His breath was foul, and the whites of his eyes beneath a fine tracery of blood-vessels were the colour of pale egg-yolk.

He twitched and jerked convulsively as though he had no control over his muscles. His clothes, what she could see of them, were torn and filthy, and an old woollen cap, which might once have been red, was jammed on to his crinkly hair.

'*Garran!*' Zanthi shrieked, scrambling backwards away from the evilly grinning face.

'Leave her alone!' Garran's voice rapped

184

out the order.

Looking over her shoulder, Zanthi's eyes widened as she saw him standing on the far side of the fire between two men, each of whom carried a rifle. The long barrels gleamed dully in the firelight.

'She has nothing to do with this.'

Zanthi couldn't see whom he was talking to. That meant there were at least four of them. She hadn't imagined it. They *had* been under surveillance.

'He lyin', boss,' the skinny youth yelled excitedly. 'An' we jest got oursels a bonus.'

'Bring her out here.' The command came from a new, more cultured voice which lacked the lilting accent prevalent among the island's poorer people.

'C'mon, missey, out you git.' The youth leaned in to grab her. Zanthi recoiled as the fetid odour of his unwashed body, overlaid with another sickly-sweet smell, assaulted her nostrils.

'Don't you touch me!' She spat the words at him and, grabbing her other boot, quickly climbed out on the far side. She started towards Garran, but one of the men beside him immediately raised his gun, and she heard the click of the safety-catch as the barrel pointed unwaveringly at her midriff. She stopped dead, bathed in a sudden cold sweat as the reality of their situation hit her with the force of a blow. Her gaze swivelled to Garran,

185

who ignored her.

'Look, you've made your point, but none of this is necessary.' Garran looked past her, addressing the man whose face she had not yet seen, his tone a blend of irritation and boredom. 'You said you wanted to talk. I'm here to talk. You have been following us for three days. You know who I am. So why the dramatics?'

Zanthi stared at him, reeling under this second shock. *He was there to talk to these criminals?* For surely they had to be outside the law, otherwise why the stealth and the weapons? Garran had known all along that they were being followed, but he hadn't told her. *Why not?*

'What is this?' she demanded, trying desperately to control the sick horror writhing in her stomach. 'What's going on?'

Garran gave his head a brief shake and his eyes flashed an urgent warning, but before she could even begin to work out what he was trying to tell her, the skinny youth loped forward, grabbed her arm, and hauled her round.

'You know who she is, boss?' Excitement had made him even more jittery. 'Dis here's ol' Fitzroy's daughter! Ain't she a pretty sight?' He leered again.

Zanthi wrenched her arm free. 'Take your hands off me,' she hissed at him, rage momentarily conquering her churning fear.

The youth jerked, his whole body twitching in small, disconnected spasms. He shifted from one foot to the other. Then, in the space of a heartbeat, his precarious mood lurched from petulance to viciousness. 'You don' talk to me like that, bitch!' His hand flashed to the back of his belt and reappeared clasping a knife with a long, finely honed blade. He flipped it over, an insane grin lighting his face, then made a feinting lunge. Zanthi flinched back.

'*Joey!*' The cultured voice was a whipcrack. The youth froze, then lowered his arm, his expression sullen and resentful. His nervous fidgeting was more pronounced than ever.

Zanthi could feel the scream building up inside her. *She must not let go.* Biting the inside of her lip so hard that she tasted the warm saltiness of blood, she turned her back on the youth in studied contempt. It was a risk, and the skin between her shoulder-blades crawled. But it was also her only protection. If the youth once realised the true extent of her fear, she was lost. She faced the man in charge.

Of average height and solidly built, he was dressed in combat jacket and trousers of drab olive-green. Gloves covered his hands, and his head and face were hidden by a black, close-fitting hood. Only his eyes were visible. Reflecting the glow of the fire like a mirror, they were utterly devoid of warmth or compassion. An icy chill pervaded Zanthi. This was a man for whom the end justified the means. He would stop at nothing to get what he wanted. But what *did* he want?

Her brain raced. The jigsaw began to fit together. Continued protests and demonstrations that developed into riots were rarely spontaneous. More often, they were carefully orchestrated by faceless men behind the scenes, men who manipulated genuine grievances for their own selfish reasons, who cared nothing for the people they professed to represent, but sought power for its own sake. Men like this one. *And Garran?*

Zanthi felt as though she were dying inside. Garran had known about these men. He had calmly admitted he had come here to talk to them. That was the real reason he had begun the survey on this side of the island, to give them plenty of time to ascertain that he was the man they expected. But what did they want to talk about? And why had he insisted on bringing her?

'So,' the smooth, cynical voice broke into her shocked bewilderment, 'what would you say you're worth, Miss Fitzroy?'

Realisation dawned. Of *course.* Driven to the limits of endurance by the stresses with her family, the demands of her job, the emotional upheaval of being with Garran, plus all the unanswered questions that surrounded him, Zanthi's control finally snapped. She began to laugh. As her shoulders shook with incipient hysteria, huge tears of despair welled up,

188

spilled over, and rolled down her cheeks. It was her heart's blood she was weeping.

He had even warned her. *Hasn't it ever occurred to you how vulnerable you are?* That really had been a stroke of genius, convincing her he really was beginning to care. What else had he said? 'Everyone is allowed one mistake.' So where did that leave her? In a class of her own. Dupe of the decade. Sucker of the century. The business with Jeremy paled into insignificance beside this. She was a mobile disaster, an accident looking for a place to happen.

Her body racked by tearing sobs, her features contorted in a bitter travesty of a smile, she raised her head, tilting her chin proudly as she bestowed a look of utter contempt on Garran. No wonder he had professed such interest and concern for her father.

Garran's eyes widened in alarm. 'No, Zanthi, don't—' He started forward, but the men on either side of him were too quick. The barrel of one gun rammed into his stomach, exploding his breath in a grunt of agony, while the butt of the other caught him a glancing blow on the jaw.

A tremor shook her and she closed her eyes. She felt the pain as if it were her own. The plantation had been her father's life. Already it had cost him dearly. She would not, could not, add to his burden.

189

'What am I worth?' She turned to the terrorist. 'Absolutely nothing.' She swayed. 'So, if you were planning to hold me for ransom, you might as well forget it. My father wouldn't give you a cent. D'you hear me? Not a single penny.' The trees were closing in and the ground kept rising and falling. 'We quarrelled, you see . . .' Why wouldn't her mouth work properly? 'And he . . .' Her voice trailed off and she was falling . . . Blackness enfolded her.

*   *   *

With awareness came pain. Her head ached, and when she tried to move her ribs hurt. She felt stiff and bruised. *What had happened to her? Where was she?*

As she sat up, she clutched at her stomach, groaning involuntarily. Opening her eyes, she blinked several times and looked around. A thin, grey light filtered under the door and through the ill-fitting shutters of the small hut. Carefully, Zanthi swung her legs off the ancient camp-bed and stood up. With its rumpled and dirty blanket, it was the only piece of furniture the hut contained. Her throat was parched and she ran her tongue over her lips in an effort to moisten them. The sound of rain, drumming on the ground outside and on the thatched roof over her head, added to her torment. She craved water.

Stumbling to the door, she pushed and

pulled, but it did not budge. She opened her mouth to shout but, before a sound emerged, shut it again, shuddering violently. *What if her yell brought the crazy Joey?* Without the controlling influence of the man he called boss . . . Zanthi's stomach heaved and she wrapped her arms around her body, fighting the panic that washed over her in nauseating waves.

What would happen now? What would they do to her? Where was Garran? *Garran.*

Images of him flashed before her eyes: the first time she had seen him, standing in the garden at Government House. Shirtsleeves rolled up, tie loosened, jacket hooked over his shoulder. Then that same evening, darkly handsome in formal dress. Already he had had her off-balance, drawing her under his subtle spell. She saw him as he had been at the cave, stripped to the waist, his hair wet from the sea, cooking breakfast for them both. Unbearable pain knifed through her. *No wonder he had seemed preoccupied.*

She had sensed from the beginning that there was far more to him than appeared on the surface, many things he had not told her. But she would never have imagined . . . not this.

Her thoughts leapt forward. She recalled his reluctance to kiss her, and the electrifying effect on them both when he did, his determination to limit their relationship, and the reason he gave, 'I have a job to do.' She had believed she understood *and he had told her she didn't.* Yet the chemistry between them had been undeniable. She had been so sure he felt as she did. Hadn't he hinted as much? She had fallen in love with him. But whatever he felt for her had not been strong enough to stop him going through with his plans. Was she *really* no more to him than bait?

Zanthi clasped her bent head in her hands, rocking back and forward. Her physical hurts were nothing compared to the anguish lacerating her soul.

She heard footsteps outside, and low voices. Terror flooded through her, turning her legs to jelly. She backed away until the rough wooden wall was behind her and she could go no further. A padlock was unfastened and a chain rattled through metal rings. Then the door opened and light flooded into the hut making her blink. The rain was a thick, grey curtain. One of the guards appeared in the doorway carrying a tin mug full of water.

As she came forward, he thrust it into her hands and, avoiding her eye, turned to go.

'Wait! *I know you,*' Zanthi gasped. 'Don't you remember? I brought food and medicine to the Reservation when your family was ill.'

The guard hesitated, his hand on the door. Then he raised his head, his gaze defiant. 'I don' remember. An', if I do, it don' make no diff'rence. What for I be grateful? My boy die. You people got plenty food and medicines, you

192

got clothes for your children, and hospitals and schools. You all got jobs and fine houses, and you take all dis t'ings as your right. An' us? What we got? *Nuthin'!* We don' even got hope.'

Zanthi winced as the truth of his statement hit home.

'But keeping me prisoner won't help you. It won't change anything,' she cried desperately as the guard closed the door behind him.

There were shouts, a commotion of sounds and voices. The door was yanked open again and Zanthi started violently as Garran stumbled in, prodded hard by the second guard's gun-barrel. Just before the door was slammed shut, cutting off the light, Zanthi glimpsed a purple bruise surrounding his left eye and cheekbone, and a swelling on his jaw.

'Oh, my God,' she whispered. None of this made sense. He was on *their* side, wasn't he? So why had they beaten him up?

Garran sat down wearily on the camp-bed, which creaked under his weight. Head bent, his hands hanging loosely between his knees, he looked exhausted. 'Have you got a death-wish or something?' he grated. Though ragged, his voice still held enough venom to make her shrink away.

Zanthi's eyes were adjusting to the gloom and she stared at him in total confusion. 'What are you talking about?'

He turned his head slowly to look at her, the movement an obvious effort. 'Joey was all for

193

killing you and dumping your body in one of the craters.'

Zanthi's breath caught in her throat.

'You were so busy being clever, telling them that you were financially worthless. Didn't it occur to you that without a ransom they had no reason to keep you alive?'

'B-but they h-had n-no reason to *k-kill* me!' she stuttered. *This wasn't happening: it was a nightmare.*

He snorted in exasperation. 'You're a *liability*. What other reason do they need?' He pushed both hands through his hair, then rubbed his face. 'You are damn lucky that I managed to convince Lezard that killing a high-ranking Government official, especially a woman, would blow their case sky-high and they would lose all public sympathy. But it's not over yet. You are alive only because Lezard still has Joey under control.'

'He's mad, insane,' Zanthi whispered.

'He's on drugs,' Garran said flatly.

'Then why does Lezard keep him around?'

Garran sighed in exasperation. 'Lezard is his supplier. In return for regular fixes, Joey does Lezard's dirty work. For him killing is the ultimate high, and he's targeted you. You represent a world he can never belong to. It wouldn't be a quick death.'

'*Stop it!*' Zanthi croaked, swallowing hard.

'Then, for God's sake, you stop handing them the excuses they're looking for!' Garran

194

snarled.

'But I *didn't*—'

'You think yelling at the guard that keeping you prisoner won't change anything, gives them an incentive to treat you *well?* They have nothing left to lose, Zanthi. Twice, I tried to warn you. Why didn't you *listen?*'

She began to shake. It was too much. 'Don't you *dare* take that tone with me!' She was almost incoherent with fury. 'You knew what was going on, I didn't. You came out here *intending* to meet these people, but you didn't bother to tell me. I hadn't volunteered for this trip, you insisted I came. If I wasn't bait, then what the hell *was* I? *Why did you bring me?*' She broke off, her chest heaving, breathless and dizzy with the force of her anger.

Garran glared at her for a moment, then, lowering his head, began to massage his temples. 'Come here and sit down before you fall down,' he said quietly.

'I wouldn't share that bed with you—'

'I didn't ask you to *sleep* with me,' cut in Garran acidly, stopping her in mid-flow. 'For one thing I'm too bloody tired to do either of us justice, and for another there are a few things we have to sort out. Don't argue, Zanthi,' he warned as she drew herself up. 'There isn't time.'

Seething, knowing he was right, that she was near the end of her tether, she stalked over to the bed and perched on the edge as far from

195

him as possible. But she couldn't maintain that posture without placing an unbearable strain on her already sore muscles. Suddenly there was a lump in her throat and she found herself fighting an overwhelming urge to cry. With trembling hands she raised the mug to her mouth. The metal clattered against her teeth and she had difficulty in swallowing. After a couple of gulps, she lowered the mug, clasping it tightly in both hands. 'I trusted you.' Harsh and strained, her voice brimmed with hurt and accusation.

He did not move. 'And you don't any more?'

The silence stretched. 'I don't know.' It was a broken whisper.

'Some trust,' he muttered.

'That's rich, coming from you!' she flared. 'Who are you, anyway?'

He didn't answer immediately and, in the silence, Zanthi sensed issues being considered, consequences weighed and decisions reached. 'Could I have some of that water?' he asked softly.

Without looking up, Zanthi passed the mug to him. As he took it, his fingers brushed hers, whether by accident or design she didn't know and was beyond caring, for it was as if she had touched bare wires. The shock was like an electric charge and she tingled all over. *It hadn't changed.* Despite everything. How could that be?

Shame and an inner turmoil at her body's

treachery deepened her flush and, though she sensed his probing gaze, she stared resolutely, if blindly, at her clasped hands.

'I *am* a surveyor, Zanthi. My qualifications are genuine.'

'But that's not all you are.'

'No,' he agreed.

She looked at him. 'Well?'

'I'm not at liberty—'

'Spare me that, Garran.' She could not keep the scathing edge from her tone. 'After all that's happened—' Her hand strayed to her ribs, as if exploration of the soreness and bruising would provide answers. Her short, tremulous laugh revealed desperation and fear. 'I don't even *know*—'

'It's all right,' he cut in, his tone definite, reassuring. 'Nothing did happen to you, not in that sense.'

She glanced up, longing to believe him.

Would I lie to you? The echo, faint and distorted, hung in the air between them.

'Except—' He hesitated, and she stopped breathing. 'I had to knock you out.'

'What?' she gasped. 'How?'

'Pressure point in your neck, while I was pretending to try to rouse you from your faint.' His tone was matter-of-fact rather than apologetic and Zanthi detected an underlying note of ruthlessness which lifted the hairs on the back of her neck. 'I had no choice. It was obvious you weren't in the right frame of mind to respond to any hints or leads from me. Lezard is no fool. He knows the Government would never agree to pay ransom money for you. They simply could not afford to. It would set a precedent for any lunatic fringe group to start kidnapping public figures, demanding huge sums to let them go. His only chance of raising more cash to fund his operations, other than by robbery, is from someone like your father. If you had convinced him that your father wouldn't pay, he'd have given you to Joey.'

Zanthi's stomach tightened.

'So I kept you unconscious *and silent* until we got here.'

She moistened her lips. 'Where are we?'

'My guess is the western edge of the Reservation.'

'Your guess?'

He shrugged, flexing his shoulders painfully. 'It was dark.'

Zanthi shivered. If he was correct, they were almost in the centre of the island, an area shunned by all islanders, densely forested, drenched by incessant rain, the ground broken by hidden craters and fissures that breathed poisonous gases into the steamy atmosphere. A place shrouded in superstition and fear, ideal for a terrorist hideout.

Her forehead creased in concentration as she tried to assimilate all he was telling her. 'How *did* we get here? In the Shogun?'

Garran shook his head and gave a huge yawn. Pushing the mug into her hand, he eased himself down on his side. 'We walked.'

'But—'

'Not you,' he said, yawning again. 'I carried you.' His voice faded. 'Fireman's lift . . .' he mumbled ' . . . no padding, sorry . . .' Making a visible effort, he roused himself, eyelids heavy. 'Need an hour, that's all . . .' His eyes closed and, within moments of sinking back on to the crumpled blanket, his deep, steady breathing told Zanthi he was dead to the world.

She stared at him for several seconds. Rousing herself, she carefully placed what was left of the precious water on the floor by the wall, then returned to the camp-bed.

'I carried you.' Over and over again the words resounded in her head. She rubbed her midriff gently. How far had he walked in the dark, up slippery, snaking mountain paths, a rifle in his back and her across his shoulder? Even more important, why had he done it?

She owed him more than her life, for if Lezard *had* given her to Joey . . . nausea overwhelmed her and her mind refused to contemplate the unspeakable horrors from which death would have been a welcome and merciful release. Crouching, she unlaced Garran's mud-caked boots and eased them off. Ignoring the pain, she lifted his legs on to the bed. His trousers were damp and gritty with earth. There was a strangling tightness in her throat as she drew a corner of the blanket over him.

She sat down on the floor, curling her legs under her. Chin on her palm, her elbow supported by the canvas-covered frame of the camp-bed, she gazed at the sleeping man.

Even in the dim light she could see, in addition to the bruising, dark shadows beneath his eyes, and lines of strain etched by physical exhaustion between his brows and bracketing his mouth.

He had driven himself to the limit of his strength carrying her here. Though he could hardly have stood by and let them kill her. Why not? If he was one of them she was far more of a threat to him alive. But if he was one of them, why had he protected her? Why had they beaten him up and locked him in here with her?

If he wasn't one of them, then who was he? Why had he come to Jumelle? He was obviously a substitute for Andrew Hemmings, the original surveyor. But who had arranged the swap, and why?

So many questions, each one spawning more. Round and round they went. Yet underneath them all was the knowledge, like a single star in a midnight sky, that even now, after all she had been through, knowing he had misled her, used her for purposes of his own and gambled with her life, there was still something between them she had never felt with any other human being. Is this what love is? she wondered. She knew then that her initial reaction on seeing him with the terrorists had been born of fear. But if what she felt for Garran Crossley was love, fear had no place in it. She had to trust him. How easy it was to say and how hard to do. If she was wrong—Yes, but if she was *right* and there were sound reasons for what he had done, and if she didn't give him the benefit of the doubt and trust him, she would have forfeited something priceless, something she would never find again as long as she lived.

So deeply immersed was she in her thoughts it was several seconds before she realised he was awake and watching her.

His face was expressionless, his gaze steady. But something had changed. All her senses quickened. It was not only her: there was something different in him.

She waited, silent, unmoving.

Raising his right hand, he stroked her head, his palm warm against her ear as he cupped her face. His gaze was intent and his eyes glistened. Zanthi's own vision blurred and wordlessly she turned her face and kissed his palm.

Earlier he had asked, 'Do you want to leave? From here the going gets tougher.'

'Not a chance,' she had replied. That kiss had been his acknowledgement and acceptance. Now she was returning it. *Would he understand what she was telling him?*

'Zanthi,' he whispered hoarsely, and compressed his lips.

Twin teardrops spilled over her lower lashes. She turned to look at him again and he gently wiped her cheek with his thumb. She shrugged helplessly and the corners of her mouth quivered. 'You brought me, you take me home, OK?' She met his gaze, and what she read there made her heart swell until she thought it would burst.

'You—' he had to clear the huskiness from his throat—'you've got yourself a deal.' His started to sit up but she stopped him, pressing her hand gently to his chest. 'Rest while you can.'

He lay back with a wry smile. 'All right, fire away.'

She hesitated. There was so much she wanted to know. Deciding what was imperative and what could wait wasn't easy, especially as she had no idea how much or how little time they had together before Lezard sent someone for them. She chose her words with care. 'How did you get involved with Lezard and . . . the others?' She shuddered at a fleeting mental picture of Joey's crazed eyes, his leering grin and twitching limbs as he taunted her with the knife.

'I'm not involved in the sense that I think you mean,' he reassured her. 'I established contact with Lezard through intermediaries before I arrived on Jumelle. My job as a surveyor provides excellent cover for establishing lines between different factions, before both sides become too deeply entrenched and the country is threatened with a coup or civil war.'

Zanthi's eyes widened. 'Who *do* you work for?'

'The survey company is my own, and very lucrative it is, too. Last year our turnover—'

'*Garran!*' Zanthi warned.

His wry grimace acknowledged her determination and admitted defeat. 'I am occasionally employed by a small department of Her Majesty's Government, tucked away between the Home and Foreign Offices. I suppose you could call me a civil servant, rather like you.'

Her expression made it clear she didn't see any similarity at all. 'Speaking of me—'

'Why did I drag you into this?' he finished for her. Sitting up, he swung his feet on to the floor and stood up. Pushing one hand into his pocket, he rubbed the back of his neck with the other. 'Pure selfishness,' he said abruptly.

She frowned up at him. 'I don't understand.'

Sitting down again, Garran drew her up on to the bed beside him and took both her hands in his. 'I tried to convince myself the reasons were all professional,' he said quietly. 'I did need an assistant, and taking you with me on the survey certainly strengthened my cover.

Don't forget, no one at Government House knew the real reasons I was here.'

'Reasons? There was more than one?'

He nodded. 'The first was to make contact with whoever was behind the riots. The second was to find out why the situation wasn't being accurately reported through normal diplomatic channels.'

Zanthi recalled his skilful probing and questioning, so subtly disguised that if the attraction between them had not been so powerful and her awareness so heightened, she might not have realised it was happening.

'But the truth was,' his gaze fell to her hands, imprisoned in his, 'I wanted to know you better. When I turned up at your flat, I was already beginning to think you were something special. After watching you deal with Hyacinth, then sail through that dinner as though you hadn't a care in the world, I *knew* you were.' He rubbed the backs of her hands with his thumbs, but Zanthi sensed he was not even aware of doing it. 'The quickest way of *really* getting to know someone is to take them out of their normal environment. A person's reactions to the unexpected, to discomfort and stress, will tell you more in minutes than you'd learn in weeks of conversation.'

'Oh, really,' Zanthi responded crisply, not sure how she felt. It sounded so calculated, and yet . . .

'You have every right to be angry.' His tone

was sober. 'Apart from the fact that I allowed personal feelings to interfere with a professional assignment—' he glanced up at her—'something which has never happened to me before—what's even worse is that, in doing so, I exposed you to terrible danger.'

Zanthi saw that he was more deeply disturbed than his controlled tone would admit. 'I'm *glad* I came,' she said quietly, stating the simple truth. 'Mind you,' she added with a spark of defiance, 'I would have preferred knowing what I was getting embroiled in!'

'If I'd had the faintest idea—The fact that Joey recognised you was appalling bad luck, but the possibility that one of them might should have occurred to me—' He broke off, the brief angry shake of his head telling her it would be a long time before he forgave himself. 'Lezard's behaviour was a shock too,' he admitted. 'My information was that they were eager for a settlement.'

'What do you think went wrong?' Zanthi asked.

'Who knows? Lezard might be fighting for his own survival. There's no such thing as honour among thieves. In any case, situations like these are always a gamble. A settlement demands genuine commitment between both parties. All too often, one side jacks up the price, demanding impossible concessions, threatening to pull out if they're not met. The other side screams blackmail, and the whole deal collapses.'

'Do you think that's what happened here?'

Garran shook his head thoughtfully. 'I'm not sure. I think Lezard has developed a taste for power and doesn't want to give it up.'

An icy chill shivered down Zanthi's spine. Her first glimpse of those cold eyes had given her the same impression.

'I've also got a feeling that there could be someone else involved, maybe not directly, but the unrest could not have attained its present level without raising the alarm in the Home Office unless . . .' He allowed the sentence to trail off, but Zanthi picked up the trend of his thoughts immediately.

She stiffened. 'You mean—someone deliberately suppressing information? But who? And why?'

CHAPTER TEN

Garran looked up suddenly, his whole body taut. Motioning her to remain silent, he left the bed and crossed the floor swiftly, light as a cat on his stockinged feet.

Infected by his sudden tension, Zanthi caught her breath. Anxiety quickened her heartbeat. What now?

Some time during the last hour the rain had

stopped. The forest was strangely silent. Zanthi listened, straining to hear, as the sound of raised voices reached her. One was Lezard's. She could not define the words but his tone was one of anger and refusal. The other voice was Joey's. Its whine held a desperation that sent unease slithering through Zanthi like an uncoiling snake.

Garran began to tug and push at the door. There was an urgency about him that frightened her.

'What is it? What's happening?' she whispered.

Ignoring her, he slapped the door with the heel of his hand, calling to the guard, his voice pitched low.

The sound of the quarrel was getting louder, Lezard alternating between firmness and reason, Joey growing even more shrill and demanding. Unable to sit still any longer, Zanthi stood up and her foot kicked over one of Garran's boots. Bending, she grabbed them both, offering them to him as he glanced round. He put them on quickly, straightening up as the chain rattled and light spilled into the airless hut.

Cradling his rifle, the guard peered in suspiciously. 'What you want?'

'You hear what's going on?' Garran demanded with the same controlled urgency which had characterised his whole manner since his attention had been caught.

The guard glanced towards the source of the noise. 'Sure. They like that alla time.' But there was a trace of unease in his expression.

'No.' Garran's voice held certainty. 'This is different. You know it. Lezard is losing control of Joey. You've got to let us go!'

'Is you mad, man?' the guard sneered. 'You know what they do to me if I do that?'

'*Listen to them!*' Garran hissed, commanding the man's full attention.

Lezard's voice rose suddenly, first in warning, then in fear. There was a crash of breaking furniture. Joey was screaming, a high-pitched squeal of demented rage. Raw panic thinned Lezard's voice as he shouted for the guards.

Zanthi heard the sound of running feet and a babble of shouts and questions. Then a blood-curdling shriek chilled her to the marrow, making her skin crawl and the fine hair on her arms lift. A burst of automatic gunfire rent the air, followed by a sharp cry and the thud of a falling body. The guard's face turned the colour of putty as Joey's insane laughter rang out above the startled squawking of the birds, high in the forest canopy.

'*Think*, man,' Garran urged. 'Once Joey has pumped himself full of dope, who will be safe? He's beyond reason, his mind has gone. Get out of here! Go back to your family.'

There was another burst of gunfire, another scream of laughter. Visibly torn, the guard glanced towards the noise. The momentary lapse of concentration was all Garran needed. Before Zanthi realised what was happening, the guard had crumpled unconscious to the ground.

Garran seized her hand. 'Keep down, and don't look back,' he urged. Then they were running, out of the hut, through the undergrowth and into the gloom of the forest.

Run. Zanthi's heart pounded, the hammering so loud that it nearly deafened her. Her breath rasped in her throat and an iron band of agony tightened around her ribs. But, though the ache in her legs was excruciating, terror lent wings to her feet. *Keep running.*

She was under no illusion as to what would happen if Joey caught up with them. In killing Lezard he had severed his one remaining link with sanity. With little to lose before, there was nothing at all to restrain him now. Stumbling and skidding on the wet, sloping ground, she pushed aside the vines and aerial roots hanging like thick strands of spaghetti from branches high above their heads and looped across their path. Even the forest seemed to be trying to trap them. Zanthi had a terrifying image of a living net of lianas and creepers, like a gigantic spider's web, closing in on her, and she fought down a choking scream. Fern fronds whipped her face and arms and serrated palm-leaves snagged her clothes as Garran dragged her after him.

Sweat soaked her shirt, plastering it to her body as she strained to breathe. *She couldn't get enough air.* Drops ran into her eyes, stinging, blinding her. She blinked, shaking her head to clear the red fog that was clouding her vision.

'*Garran*,' she sobbed, 'I c-can't—' Her foot caught in a root and her hand was wrenched from his as she crashed full-length to the ground.

She sprawled, her face against the damp earth, painfully winded, unable to move, her whole body trembling, her mind aware of nothing but the necessity of getting oxygen into her starved lungs.

'Come on, Zanthi, get up!' The urgent command seemed to come from a long way off, almost drowned by the racing clamour of her heartbeat. He was lifting her, pulling her to her feet.

'No—no, I can't.' Her throat burned, her mouth and lips were parched.

'You can and you must!' His voice was harsh, remorseless. 'We have to keep moving. There'll be time to rest when you get home. Think about home, Zanthi!' She was on her feet, her legs like india-rubber. 'Visualise it in your mind's eye, the colours you chose, the pattern on those big squashy cushions, the pictures on the wall. Can you see them?' A strong arm around her shoulders was holding her up, guiding her forward, firm and insistent.

210

'Can you smell the jasmine on the balcony? That's better, a little faster now, you're doing fine.'

After a while she no longer trembled and she had stopped staggering. She was finding a rhythm. Her breathing was less painful, though her heart still thudded against her ribs like a captive demanding to be set free. With each step Garran pushed her a little harder, silently urging more speed.

'How far is it to the clearing?' she croaked at last, all her efforts focused on putting one foot in front of the other, keeping the rhythm, moving faster, getting away.

'We're not going back to the clearing. Keep going!' Garran's voice sharpened as her stride faltered.

'B-but—all your valuable survey equipment '

'That is replaceable,' he answered brusquely. 'You are not. Joey will expect us to make for the Shogun. It's the first place he'll look.'

Zanthi swallowed. 'Then how do we get out of here?'

'By the quickest route.' His voice held a grimness that bothered Zanthi. She looked up at him and her sharp intake of breath made a tiny, hissing sound. His bruised face, tousled hair, black beard-stubble and muddy sweat-stained clothes added to the aura of ruthless determination emanating from him.

'We're going down Diablo,' he stated flatly

in a tone that permitted neither argument nor discussion.

Zanthi kept her head down, concentrating fiercely on her boots, her skin tingling as though an army of ants were crawling over it. Walk, *don't think*. If she didn't think, she couldn't be afraid. Down Diablo!

Garran's fingers tightened their grip on her shoulder, making her wince. 'It will be all right, Zanthi,' he promised. 'I'll get you home. We've got a deal, remember?'

She nodded, trying to smile, not trusting herself to speak. *Devil River.*

They headed south-west, managing to avoid the craters, warned by the pungent smell that stung their throats and made their eyes water. They scrambled over rocky passes and waded through swamps where mangrove trees perched on spidery, aerial roots and clouds of insects hummed above the stagnant pools.

Garran fashioned cone-like cups from glossy leaves and scooped rainwater from a low palm whose crown of leaves formed a reservoir. It slid down Zanthi's throat like nectar. They found bananas, wild limes and berries, and ate as they walked, while Zanthi drew on reserves of strength she had not known she possessed.

Or maybe, she reasoned, her mind simply wasn't capable of sustaining the level of fear that had overwhelmed her.

There had been one nasty moment when,

with eyes widening, face chalk-white, she had been sure she heard voices and the creak and swish of trampled undergrowth. But Garran had forced her on, telling her it was only the birds and the wind in the canopy overhead. She wasn't sure that she believed him, but kept her doubt to herself and quickened her pace.

An hour passed, then another, and gradually, no longer blanking out everything but survival, her brain began working again and she found herself mulling over all that Garran had told her. She understood now the feeling of distance which had been one of the first things she noticed about him. She had quickly recognised his ability to draw people out, unobtrusively coaxing them into saying far more than they'd intended, while revealing almost nothing of himself. But, though aware, she had not been able to prevent herself falling victim to it.

Even now, in so many ways he was still a stranger to her, yet she loved him.

How confused she had been the night of the dinner, angry, scared and exhilarated all at once. Her whole life had changed that day. It would be strange going back. She wasn't the same person any more. Garran's arrival had opened her eyes to so much she had tried to avoid seeing.

Her mind ranged back over recent weeks, recalling the changed atmosphere at Government House: the Governor's lack of interest in matters of state, his preoccupation with the garden, and his obsession with trivial details concerning social events.

'Oh, no!' she said aloud.

Garran looked round. 'What is it?'

She turned her face up to his, strain tightening her forehead. 'I've been thinking—what you said about someone suppressing information. It couldn't be just—well—accidental, could it?' Even to herself it was obvious she was clutching at straws. 'I can't believe it's deliberate, not Sir James! I know he's not been himself lately, but—'

'It's not accidental,' Garran said firmly. 'But nor is the Governor behind it. I don't think Sir James realises what's happening. He's a sick man, Zanthi. Hadn't you noticed?' His tone was a combination of surprise and censure.

'Yes,' she admitted. 'Margaret and I both wondered, but Paul brushed it off and we were so busy . . .' She was silent for a moment considering all the implications. Then she looked up again. 'But if His Excellency isn't involved—No one else has access to the secrets room and all the files and reports—' She broke off as realisation hit her.

'Except the Governor's ADC, Lieutenant Paul Benham,' Garran finished for her.

Zanthi stared at him, then followed automatically, no longer conscious of their grinding pace, or of the forest around them, the sunbeams angling down like golden

214

spotlights. 'But what reason would he have to do such a thing?'

Garran's stride did not falter. He glanced at her over his shoulder. 'You probably know him as well as, if not better, than, anyone else at Government House. What drives him? What is his motivating force? Money?'

Zanthi shook her head. 'No. Ambition.' She was startled by the swiftness and certainty of her reply. 'He has already made sure of a glowing recommendation from Lady Fiona.' Her tone was clipped, blending contempt for Paul with a mixture of shock and sympathy for the Governor's wife. 'Paul is not a man to leave such matters to chance.'

'So the last thing he wants is for anything to reach the Home Office which puts a question mark over the Governor's ability to handle the current situation,' Garran pointed out. 'As for his reasons, I can only presume he feels the shadow would fall on him too and damage his chances of promotion.' Garran's tone was scathing. 'Benham does not want his own little boat rocked.'

Zanthi was incredulous. 'You really think that he'd sacrifice Sir James's health and Jumelle's security for that?' She didn't give him the chance to answer, as her thoughts sped on. 'But what about Lady Fiona? Surely she can see—'

'Put yourself in her place,' Garran sounded surprisngly gentle. 'Her husband's career has been hers, too. She has no family, no grandchildren to fill the gap that retirement will bring. After a lifetime of service and support, a life crammed with people and social events, there are only a few months left to go. If she can just prop Sir James up, cover for him, and maintain appearances, they will retire in style, fêted and acclaimed and high on every society hostess's party list. They'll be able to dine out every night for the rest of their lives.'

'But,' blurted out Zanthi, 'if Sir James doesn't get the medical attention he needs, he could be dead before—' She stopped, stunned by the enormity of Paul's selfishness. He, more than anyone else, had been in a position to warn Lady Fiona that the charade could not continue, that the Governor needed expert help *before it was too late.* But he had done nothing. 'What about Jumelle? Will the demonstrations and riots stop, now Lezard is dead?'

Garran shook his head. 'I doubt it. There may be a lull, but the basic cause of the unrest still exists: lack of land, food and jobs for the poor. If the problem is not tackled quickly another self-styled "liberator" will jump in to take Lezard's place.'

She swallowed. 'You don't think Joey?'

'He won't live long enough.' Garran's voice held a cold detachment that reminded her, more forcibly than anything else could have, how different his life had been from hers. How

216

much more he had done and seen, how much farther he had travelled in body, mind and emotions.

Suddenly she was aware of the yawning gulf of experience that separated them, and with the awareness came fear. It bore no resemblance to the mouth-drying terror Joey had inspired. This was an icy, numbing dread.

Knowing Garran had lifted her into a new realm of existence. He was challenge, comfort, tyrant, teacher and friend. In just a few short days he had become the core of her reason for living. Without him she would survive, but never again would she be whole.

But what of his feelings for her? He was drawn to her, and the initial attraction had broadened and deepened during their trip. He had promised to get her home safely and she knew that he would risk his own life to keep his word. But what was his driving force? Love? *Or Guilt.*

She lifted her gaze from the faint narrow trail that they had picked up, and regarded the tall, broad-shouldered-figure walking several strides ahead of her. Let him love me, she prayed silently.

Suddenly he stopped, his arm outstretched to keep her back.

Her heart gave a painful kick. 'What's the matter?' she whispered.

He glanced round, his eyes gleaming as they met hers. 'Can't you hear it?'

Frowning with concentration, she listened intently. Then, very faintly, she detected a low rumble, overlaid by a rushing sound. *Water.* As her eyes widened, he drew her to his side, his arm encircling her shoulders. A fleeting weakness at his touch was followed by an infusion of strength. They were together now, and tomorrow was a lifetime away.

She looked up at him. 'How far—' she began, then gasped as he pushed aside the foliage in front of them and led her forward a couple of steps.

They were on the edge of a cliff. A hundred metres below, the river cascaded over jagged rocks and plunged into a blue-black pool which curved out of sight around a fern-draped wall.

'*Diablo*,' Zanthi breathed, and a shiver raised gooseflesh on her bare arms. Then, from the depths of the forest behind them, came a faint brief stutter of gunfire.

Garran's face tightened, and his eyes, as Zanthi's whole body jerked with shock, were as black and hard as jet.

'Come on!' He seized her hand and started along the cliff edge.

'Where?' panted Zanthi.

'We must get down to the river.'

'We *can't!*' she cried. 'Not—' She looked over the edge and closed her eyes, feeling nausea churn her stomach.

'It's not as steep as it looks,' he tried to reassure her. 'The trail led here, so there must be a way down.'

'Garran—'

He turned and, gripping her shoulders, shook her. 'It's the river or Joey,' he said brusquely. 'Make your choice.'

Without waiting for a reply, he grabbed her hand again and pushed through the shrubs and ferns which grew right up to the cliff edge.

'I thought so.' There was quick satisfaction in his voice. 'Watch where I put my feet, Zanthi, and don't look down.'

'Garran, I—' Her voice was a strangled. plea.

He turned to her, his gaze steady, his tone gentle. 'Didn't I promise that I'd get you home safely?' She nodded, beyond speech. 'Do you trust me?' She swallowed, then nodded again. 'Then what are you worried about?'

She stared at him for several seconds, felt the powerful force of his indomitable will, then, as his face cracked in a grin, she gave an exaggerated shrug and grimaced. 'Worried?' Her teeth chattered. 'Who's worried?'

The look in his eyes brought a warm glow to her cheeks and infused her with determination. She would make it, *somehow*. He moved fractionally, and she swayed towards him and just for an instant she thought, *hoped desperately*, that he was going to kiss her. But he turned quickly away, his jaw tightening, and stepped over the edge of the cliff.

Zanthi had no idea how long it took to

reach the bottom. One minute she was scrabbling for handholds among the crevices and the vegetation that clung to the rock face, with her adrenalin pumping, hands scratched and bleeding, leg muscles quivering with the strain, and the next she had slithered down the last few metres into Garran's arms and he was holding her so tightly she could hardly breathe.

She clung to him, relief and reaction making her head swim.

Then, abruptly, he released her and, keeping his head averted, turned and set off downstream over the tumbled rocks that lined the river's edge.

The pool was deep, the surface smooth. Only an oily dimple near the centre marked the strength of the current. Tiny round snails clung to rocks worn smooth by the constant flow. As their footsteps echoed against the canyon walls, a startled blue heron flapped heavily from a rock on the opposite side and flew away upstream.

The river widened, grew shallower, and they left the rocks to walk on sand and gravel. They rounded a bend and Zanthi felt the sun's heat on her face and blinked at its brightness.

All too soon the banks closed in again, the canyon walls soaring up, sheer and dark on either side, cutting off the sun and plunging them into deep shadow. Confined by the rock walls, the river speeded up. There was no edge of sand or boulders left on which to walk.

Garran had kept a little way ahead, forcing the pace, making her keep up. Now he stopped and waited for her. 'Can you swim?'

She nodded wearily.

'It won't be long, Zanthi. Just a few more hours and you'll be home.'

She looked up at him, but already he was gazing down the river. He seemed to be distancing himself from her and she didn't know what to do.

Garran waded in until the water reached his thighs, then beckoned her forward. 'Keep to the side and let the current carry you,' he directed, then launched himself into the smooth flow with barely a ripple. Gritting her teeth, Zanthi followed.

The shock of the cold water took her breath away and she gasped and panted, spluttering as she fought to keep her head above the water.

The gap between the towering cliffs grew smaller and the current strengthened. Zanthi could hear the thunder of a cascade up ahead. She floundered her way to the side. Suddenly, she felt a stabbing pain in her side and her shirt was grabbed. She uttered a piercing scream before the water closed over her head. Lashing out wildly, her hand touched the cold, hard, slimy surface of a submerged tree trunk. She kicked and struggled, her lungs bursting, and just as a roaring blackness threatened to engulf her, she felt herself yanked free and hauled on to one of the huge boulders that had lodged at a bend in the canyon.

Coughing and retching, trembling violently, she sucked in sweet, life-giving air.

'Are you all right?' Garran pushed her dripping hair out of her eyes, his face an expressionless mask. She nodded, still panting.

'Zanthi,' his tone was compelling, 'we must move on. Look!' He pointed.

Following his hand, she saw rain shrouding the mountains.

'It might only be a shower,' he said, 'but if it isn't . . .'

Zanthi scrambled to her feet. He didn't have to go on. Her imagination painted an all too vivid picture. A picture of rain soaking the earth until, unable to absorb any more, it crumbled and broke away, falling into the streams and brooks which within minutes would grow into foaming brown torrents. 'I'm OK,' she croaked.

He looked at her as if he was about to speak but, instead, turned away, heading downstream over the tumbled rocks. Stumbling after him, Zanthi paused for an instant to look down at the massive arc of water that gushed over the precipice to smash in a boiling froth a few metres below.

They walked, swam and walked again. Zanthi's world shrank to the next stretch of rock or sand, the next curve in the river. She shivered continuously and every muscle in her body ached. The pain gnawed at her, sapping what remained of her strength. Hardest of all to bear was Garran's withdrawal. He barely spoke except to drive her on, demanding more speed, more effort.

There was a new surge in the current and the river level was rising, the water clouded brown. As she crawled out on to the rocks once more, she was aware of a change in the light.

With an effort she raised her head. The right bank had flattened and broadened, the towering rock face reduced to a forested mound. Behind the trees the sun was setting in a blaze of flame, gold and lilac. She was utterly exhausted. God alone knew how much farther they had to go, and soon it would be dark. She sank to her knees.

At that moment, Garran glanced round. 'What the hell do you think you're doing?' he roared, striding towards her. 'Get up. Come on, get on your feet!'

Automatically, she obeyed him as she had right through the endless day. But as she straightened up, swaying and at the very limit of her endurance, something in Zanthi snapped and tears poured down her face.

'I hate you, Garran Crossley,' she screamed at him. 'You're nothing but a sadistic bully.'

He flinched as if her words were knives plunging into his flesh. But she was beyond caring. Sobbing helplessly, she watched him come towards her and closed her eyes. It didn't matter what he did now. Nothing mattered any more. She just wanted to lie down and sleep and never wake up again.

Her head jerked painfully as he grabbed her shoulders and shook her hard. 'Now, you listen to me!' he snarled through gritted teeth. 'You are not giving up now, do you hear? I know you're exhausted, *and* hungry, *and* cold. So am I. But you're *alive!* And I intend to keep you that way even if—' He broke off.

'It kills me?' she gasped, hysterical laughter choking her.

'Zanthi, we're nearly there. You have to keep going. It's not that far now.'

Her head dropped forward. 'I can't,' she whispered.

Seizing her chin, he forced her head up, his eyes blazing with a mixture of emotions she could not understand. 'You can and you will. Blame me, Zanthi, hate me all you want, but *keep bloody moving!*'

Half-dragging, half-carrying her, he crossed the slippery rocks. A stretch of gravel was traversed by small streams. Then, where the forest met the river bank, they turned on to a broad trail. Part of Zanthi's brain registered the fact that a track meant people. He hadn't lied. They were almost there. The knowledge pierced her like a double-edged sword and her grief was overwhelming. Her whole body shook with the force of her sobs.

'You did it, Garran. You kept your promise!'

224

She broke free, staggering backwards, naked misery contorting her face. 'So now you can walk away with a clear conscience. All debts discharged. The slate wiped clean.' Scalding tears brimmed over and she dashed them away with the back of her hand.

'*Walk away?*' His voice was a tormented rasp. 'Is that what you want?'

'What *I* want? Isn't it what you've been doing since the moment we escaped?' she sobbed. 'I've given everything you asked of me. I kept going longer than I ever believed I could—'

'My God,' he cried, 'don't you think I realised that? Every time I looked at you and saw how bravely you—' He broke off, his lips tightly compressed, a muscle in his jaw jumping.

'But it's not enough, is it?' Zanthi said hopelessly. 'I could never be enough.'

He stared at her, utterly still, an almost visible tension emanating from him as though he was holding himself tightly in check. 'Zanthi,' his voice reflected rigid control, 'you've got it all wrong. I'm responsible for everything you've been through. It's entirely my fault that you're here. Have you any idea how much I despise myself?'

A sob mingled with ironic laughter. 'So because you feel guilty I have to suffer even more?'

'No . . .' Confusion gave him an air of

vulnerability totally at odds with his piratical appearance. 'I never wanted to hurt you.'

She screwed up her last shreds of courage. 'Then don't leave me.'

His hands hanging loosely at his sides, Garran closed his eyes and drew in a deep, ragged breath. When he opened them again his gaze was unnaturally bright. 'Leave you?' he muttered harshly. 'I'd as soon stop breathing.'

'Oh, Garran,' Zanthi whispered, stretching out her hands to him. 'I—I—' The words would not be held back. 'I do love you.'

Enfolding her in strong arms, he stroked her tousled hair as the last rays of the setting sun flushed the western sky from pale pink to deep rose. Then he tilted her chin and gazed into her eyes. 'What did I do to deserve you, Zanthi Fitzroy?'

She smiled up at him, exhausted, wet and muddy, and filled with a radiant happiness that reduced all her aches and pains to insignificance. The next few days would be far from easy. Neither of them would have time to rest and recuperate until reports had been made, and moves to rectify the situation at Government House set in motion. But with Garran beside her, there was nothing she couldn't face.

Her eyes danced with mischief and promise. 'Oh, I expect I'll think of something.'

226